#BLP

The Pleasure Package

DENISE ESSEX

#BLP

For the dreamers and the creators

*I also dedicate this book to the readers. Thank **you** for your support. I see you!*

Visit bit.ly/readBLP to join our mailing list for sneak peeks and release day links!

B. Love Publications - where Authors celebrate black men, black women, and black love.

To submit a manuscript for consideration, email your first three chapters to blovepublications@gmail.com with SUBMISSION as the subject.

The BLP Podcast – bit.ly/BLPUncovered

Let's connect on social media!
Facebook - B. Love Publications
Twitter - @blovepub
Instagram - @blovepublications

Acknowledgments

I'd like to acknowledge:

My family: Thank you for allowing me to take up space as an author.

My publisher, B. Love the G.O.A.T., and the dopest pen sisters an author could ask for: Thank you for your advice, support, and encouragement.

CYN, Writing Coach Extraordinaire: Thank you for encouraging me to trust my pen and my skills and thank you for all of your feedback!

Editors and proofreaders: Angels sent from heaven. Thank you, Latisha, for the class, and the Facebook group! Crystal, thank you for taking time to create a video to help me with self-edits! Y'all dope AF! Thank you for your patience and all the invaluable information you share!

My accountability partners: Author Mya, Erika/Emerald B, Cecila, AJ, Odilla, Anne, and Stephanie. Thank you for motivating me with your inspiring goals and holding space for mine!

Me: Thank you for *continuing* to do it, despite your fears. I see you, Goddess!

Reader Groups: B. Love Publications Book Cove, Diem's Diamonds, and last but certainly not least, Denise Essex Sweet Heat Seekers.

Readers: Thank you for taking time from your life to play in my world!

Note from Denise

Dear reader,

Thank you for your interest in my current release. **There is a brief mention of domestic violence.** Please take care of yourself if you find this topic triggering.

If you resonate with what you read, please leave a positive review on **Amazon, Goodreads, and TikTok**. Also, be sure to share it with your friends. If you're interested in supporting me as an author, give me a like and follow on my Facebook business page, and sign up for my mailing list so we can keep in touch.

Facebook Business Page
    Mailing list

With Love,
    Denise Essex

Sweet Heat

DENISE ESSEX

One

MALIK'S SCULPTED abs and well-defined back didn't happen by accident. His consistent six a.m. runs were responsible for his mellow demeanor and his shredded physique. It had been well over a decade since his college football days, but old habits died hard. The intensity of his workouts continued beyond graduation.

Malik was at peace with the sounds of the singing birds, his breath, and the slap of his sneakers against the paved roads. The cool March air in his small Georgia town encouraged him to push himself harder before his real work began.

Malik Malone was at war with the fact that at the prime age of thirty-five, he lived at home with his mother. In his gut, he knew he'd made the right decision to accept the voluntary layoff his company offered him during the pandemic. Malik took the severance and moved back in with his parents to save money to fund his business.

As he rounded another bend on the winding country road, his thoughts drifted to his million-dollar idea. Malik had always been a muscular built man. And as a result, he struggled to find comfortable boxer briefs. If they fit in the crotch, they were loose in the thigh; if they fit around the thigh, there was still no room for his manhood. He was on a similar run over a decade ago, when he had the idea to create a line of underwear for men with his body type.

Whenever Malik thought of his company, Hood Body Briefs, he experienced physical sensations of pure bliss. He felt tingles as he continued his run and mentally dissected how his brand would meet the needs of countless people. His external reality didn't quite match the wealth that brewed on the inside of him. It was the drive to finish his final mile faster than he'd ever ran.

Malik chose to deal with the criticism of his career choices during his morning run. Though his inner circle supported him with blind faith, the other people in his life had expressed everything but encouragement. They couldn't fathom how he'd left a stable six-figure accounting job to accept a gig delivering packages. Malik could understand how it looked on the outside.

He was mentally tough, but exercise helped to reaffirm him and the goals he'd set. Sweat covered his entire body as he walked his parents' street with his hands atop his head to cool down. His breaths slowed as he wordlessly greeted an older woman who walked her dog and waved.

Malik retrieved his key for the final part of his workout. He preferred to run without music, but he'd blast his Bluetooth speaker while he lifted weights and maxed out on pushups. A smile spread across his face as the garage opened. A smoothie was propped on a shelf near his weight bench.

His fraternal twin sister, Markita, must have woken up early to prepare his protein, because she worried he went too hard with nothing on his stomach. He paired the speakers with his smartphone and selected his up-tempo trap music playlist. He'd need all the endorphins he could get for the toxic job that funded his dream.

* * *

MALIK STROLLED UNHURRIEDLY through the doors of his current employer dressed in a canary-yellow uniform. The color did nothing to enhance his looks, not that he needed any assistance. Despite the drastic shift from tailored business casual fits—at his prestigious accounting job—to a tacky delivery mandated ensemble, Malik was a striking man, no matter the clothes he wore.

The receptionist snapped her gum and threw a 'fuck me' face his way. While Malik was flattered, he was much too focused to entertain anyone he'd see beyond the moment. A coworker would be a problem, and he knew it.

"Put some pep in your step, Malone," his boss spat from his worn desk chair. Malik's boss never moved his wide ass from that damn chair. It was conveniently positioned behind a glass encased office, situated in the center of the delivery structure.

Malik took a commission-based delivery position because the hustler in him knew he could stand to make a ton of money in a short amount of time. The Glamazon delivery company was a dysfunctional organization that took advantage of the employees and those who participated in making it a trillion-dollar corporation.

Malik showed signs of an entrepreneur in elementary school. The teachers and staff decided to remove the vending machines without warning. All the complaints from the young student body fueled an idea in his underdeveloped hustler spirit. Malik saved up his allowance to buy gum from the warehouse store his parents went to each week to buy groceries in bulk.

Malik took the gum to school and sold it for double the price of what he'd paid. He knew the other students would practically spend anything because of the convenience. It was his first encounter with supply and demand.

But an adult Malik wouldn't break a sweat for his temporary job unless it directly benefited his end goal.

"I'm ten minutes early."

"You got a shit ton of deliveries because Thompson is slowing down the numbers with his sprained ankle."

Malik's supervisor, Hal, was an overweight man in his fifties. Hal got kickbacks each time their location surpassed the ever-rising quotas. He pushed his employees with questionable tactics, despite their physical limitations.

"Thompson has a doctor's note. He's here because he's afraid to get fired, not because he should be working," Malik mumbled. His cadence was slow and smothered in a thick southern drawl he refused to adjust because he was at work. Malik walked and talked at his own pace. He also wore his diamond fang grill no matter where he was.

"Don't be a hero, Malone. I need you to pick up Thompson's slack. I've given you several of his deliveries, and I expect you to have them done on time."

Malik nodded slowly. If his boss thought he'd complain, he was dead wrong. Hal had just guaranteed he'd make double his pay for the day. *Let's go!*

Malik had a pep in his step as he exited Glamazon's building at the rear. The weather had warmed, although it hadn't quite reached the height of the legendary Georgia heat. It was an ideal day to move packages and make money. Malik loaded the truck with his assigned deliveries along with Thompson's. His coworkers muttered offhanded comments about how Malik was a teacher's pet when he'd accepted Hal's challenge without pushback.

How the hell do they know about this shit already? I know I walk slow, but damn. I could've sworn I just had the conversation with Hal's old ass. He waved them off and continued with his tasks. Robert Malone was Malik's first example of a hard worker. Malik couldn't remember a time when his father missed a day of work, and yet, somehow, he was present in both his and his twin sister's lives.

Markita Malone was Malik's twin and his ride or die. She was undeniably Malik's best friend. Whenever he needed a sounding board or a safe space, she was a phone call away. Their relationship maintained an equal give-and-receive dynamic.

While she was an amazing listener, he relished his position in her life as a protective older brother. He often teased her that he was six minutes older, which made him wiser in the ways of the world. The only time he'd worried their relationship might suffer was when she got pregnant by her deadbeat baby daddy, John.

Malik couldn't stand him from the beginning. But the birth of his nephew and godson brought them closer together. John was nowhere to be found during his son's birth. Malik showed up for his sister and made a vow to be the father figure John John deserved. He cut his umbilical cord and held him while his sister slept.

Malik and his sister were raised by two parents who loved them without conditions. While they were affirmed, they were also pushed to be their best selves. Robert may have been the standard for discipline, but it was Angela who had them at story time at the library once a week, since before either of them could walk. She emphasized the importance of being able to think critically.

With all the support Malik had in his life, there was no one who cherished him more than his grandmother, Cicely Malone. She was the one who fussed at him for his complaints about his ill fitted underthings. One afternoon, she told him she was done, and he needed to get over it or do something about it. After the scolding from his biggest fan, Malik went on a run, and the idea for Hood Body Briefs was born. When he revealed his idea to the family, they all sat silently, unsure of how to conceal their concerns.

The plan was set for Malik and his sister. They were to attend college and get their degrees. He'd basically told them he would change those plans to sell underwear. While his family would never outright deter him, he was a bit before his time, and they didn't know how to catch up to his vision.

Cicely waited until everyone else cleared out and then gathered her measuring tape and sewing supplies. Malik was discouraged and curious about what his grandmother was up to. She took his measurements and made him promise to buy her one of those blush-colored luxury vehicles when he inevitably made his first million.

Along with Cicely, Malik felt he had the invisible support of his famous mentor, Taylor Dawn. Malik didn't know him personally, but he'd followed his work religiously since college. Taylor Dawn was a multimillion-dollar mogul who created and owned the Funded by Us Clothing company. Malik had all of his books and had even attended a few of his speaking engagements.

Malik watched the video of Taylor Dawn's story so many times, he'd memorized it. His continual rejection from banks—despite the popularity of the brand—his mother utilizing her home to fund his dream, then the fact that the company went on to earn billions, were all motivators for Malik to charge forward. Taylor Dawn's success was settled deep within Malik Malone's spirit. It had planted a seed he was dedicated to water.

Malik's easy smile was plastered across his face as he slammed the creaky swing doors of the company issued vehicle. His parcels were arranged in the order of his stops. His system took a bit of additional time on the front end, but the rest of his shift would progress seamlessly.

Two

"I'VE ALREADY SENT THOSE SPREADSHEETS," Claudia responded into her headset. She'd been fully dressed and ready for work since six thirty. Her director's gray, fluffy eyebrows bunched together.

"It's barely seven a.m. Did you sleep at all?" he queried.

Claudia woke at five and went for a jog around her immaculately manicured neighborhood division. She followed her morning jog with an intense online yoga Pilates fusion class. Claudia was recently promoted, and though things were never better at work, her personal life was in a word... miserable.

Her morning workouts helped her deal with the anger she held against her ex-husband, Tommy Butner. Claudia hated that name but took it because she was in love.

"LET'S GET MARRIED," *Tommy said with a look of sheer excitement spread across his youthful features.*

Claudia met Tommy Butner her first year away at college. They were convinced it was love at first sight. Tommy moved through campus unlike any other guy she'd ever met. She was taken with the way he demanded respect and carried himself like a young politician. She later learned he was the only child of the Butner empire.

The Butner family owned a fleet of high-end shopping centers in the state of Georgia. Claudia wasn't interested in his money, nor did she care about the popularity of his name. One of the first things Claudia said to Tommy was about his last name. She'd asked him what kind of name was Butner.

He was so caught off guard that she didn't know who he was, he asked to walk her home. For the next two years, they were inseparable and insanely hot and heavy. Claudia saw a future for them, but Tommy had been in a hurry to make her his wife.

Against her better judgment, Claudia replied with an unconfident, "OK." Her response to his declaration to get married came out with the unsteady inflection of a question. They were much too young to get married, and she knew it. But he was the *"Tommy Butner". What if he wouldn't wait for her? What if she wouldn't get another opportunity to be Mrs. Butner?*

To make matters worse, Claudia felt her family lost the little interest they had in her once the marriage ended. Claudia was the scapegoat in her family. She'd never done anything they felt was worthy outside of when she took on the Butner name, so to 'lose it' was unacceptable and unforgivable in their eyes.

She feared her single status had made her bitter. But instead of incessant worry, Claudia committed to keeping her body and her career tight.

She refocused on the gentleman in the square alongside hers, on the screen of the laptop, when she responded, "I did. It wasn't a problem at all."

"I have full confidence in your ability to lead your team into our best quarter yet. Let's check in at the end of the day."

"I'm looking forward to it, sir."

"Oh, Nicholas has been singing your praises. Keep up the good work, Claudia."

With a chuckle, Claudia added, "I sure will."

Nicholas was her talented and very biased mentor who'd encouraged her to take up space in the company. It was Nick who mirrored Claudia's brilliance back to her during their one-on-one check-ins and implored her to speak up in board meetings when she had ideas. In his eyes, she could do no wrong.

At times, she complained he never gave her any notes or feedback on ways she could improve. His response was the only thing she needed to focus on was her visibility within an organization that hadn't caught up to the fact it needed a voice like hers.

Claudia wrapped up her call and went about the business of slaying her workday. She effortlessly cut her to-do list down to zilch where it belonged. She was thankful for her time outdoors during her morning jog as she looked up and noted the sun was on the way to bed. The day may have been over for most, but she had one more important conference call before she could successfully end her day.

She'd worked through her lunch and had hidden her camera during a meeting to eat leftovers. Now that it was well into the evening, her stomach grumbled angrily. If everyone had prepared in advance, they could tackle this meeting efficiently, and she could sign off and go and pick up a real meal.

"The day is just getting started here," one of the men said in a loud, cheerful voice. The call was between Claudia's stateside team and their sister team in Australia. They wasted almost twenty minutes in comparison over who had what weather and who was in what time of day.

Claudia huffed and willed herself not to roll her eyes upward. Her camera was still on. It was crucial for her to be active on this call because the decisions would directly affect her team. Just as they ended the painful banter and shifted to talks of product performance, Claudia felt the picture frames on her wall shake as if she were in an earthquake.

The bass of a vehicle near her front door blared and rattled the car fiercely.

"What the hell?" Claudia muttered to herself. She connected to her headset and stopped her camera to investigate who was responsible for the awful noise. "Fucking Glamazon."

Claudia watched through the window as a Glamazon delivery man bopped from the driver's seat of his truck to the back to grab a package. He checked the package with an electronic device, all while his music continued at the same loud setting.

Claudia had had enough. She snatched open her door and yelled unsuccessfully in his direction. She couldn't be heard over the incessant thuds of the song.

He bobbed his head to the melody and strolled up to her door with his head down like he had all the time in the world. His tacky uniform burned her eyes and agitated her already bitchy mood.

"What are your thoughts, Claudia?" She heard a faint query through her device. The sound of her colleague's voice was like a whisper compared to the intrusive bellow of rap lyrics from the Glamazon truck.

"I'm having a hard time hearing with the noise in my background. Please come back to me," Claudia said. She tried her best to conceal the irritation in her voice.

"Not a problem." Her colleague continued down the line of questions with her fellow team members, as the delivery guy finally made his way up her sidewalk. She'd opened the door wider, and once he lifted his head, he let his eyes roam Claudia's body unapologetically.

Malik took in her feminine frame, accentuated by her black and white striped pencil skirt, her fitted white blouse, and her fire engine red stilettos. Her body was tight and toned, and her skin looked luminous. He could feel a desperate housewives' type of energy float off her as his mind struggled to understand how someone as fine as her wasn't out with her man at this hour. *Is she still working?*

He quickly checked and saw her ring finger was vacant. Claudia had red matte lipstick on her pouty lips, but it was the pearled chain attached to her black geometric shaped glasses that caught his eyes. *Got damn!*

"Shit," he said. His voice was deep, and that solitary word came out painfully slow. She didn't have time for this. In addition to the ungodly noise he played on the job, he wore jewelry in his mouth like a rapper.

Claudia lived her entire life in the south, but she'd never seen a grill in person. It seemed like a waste since, she had to admit, he had a nice smile. Why would he outline his teeth in diamonds? Was this his way of peacocking? Well, she wasn't interested. She was livid. How dare he disturb the peace like that.

"Watch your mouth!" she spat.

His thick ebony eyebrows hugged in response to her command, and his original smile faded instantly.

"'Scuse me?" Malik asked. He tugged at his chin hair as if it would help to calm the fire in his belly. He'd been with Glamazon for a few years and dealt with the worst of the worst in terms of customers, but never had he been spoken down to in this way.

"I don't think that's the best way to go about it," Claudia said into her headset, but with her eyes locked on Malik.

"Huh?" he asked, heated, and confused.

Claudia rolled her eyes upward. "Not you."

"Are you Claudia Vaughn Butner?" When he asked, amusement laid across his mannish features. *She definitely gets teased with a name like Butner, unless she's related to those high-falutin Butners who own the shopping centers. If that's the case, this shit all makes sense now.*

Claudia scowled and held up her finger to hush him.

Malik was more than offended by her rude behavior. "I'm a grown ass man. Don't shush me." He kissed his teeth and bent to leave her package.

"Give it to me," she commanded.

"You talkin' to me now?"

She rested a hand on her hip where her fitted pencil skirt hugged her frame. "Yes."

"OK, Ms. Butner." Malik handed her the package. "You enjoy the rest of your evening, ma'am." He'd snapped into customer service mode just before he walked off to create space from her ball busting energy.

"Hey."

"What's up?" Malik asked as he turned back in her direction. As far as he was concerned, their business was done. She was rude, and he didn't have shit else to say to her.

"You're very unprofessional."

"Is that right?" Malik crossed his muscular arms in front of his chest, then took the opportunity to pull a toothpick from his pocket as he awaited her response. Toothpicks helped to calm his nerves since he couldn't smoke on the job.

"Yes. First, your music is way too loud and much too improper for this neighborhood."

"Improper?" Malik's eyebrows rose again, and his toothpick damn near fell from his full lips. What was this woman's problem? She needed some dick, and she needed it now.

"Yes, improper. Then you walk up to my door and interrupt my business call, and you're wearing jewelry in your mouth like some sort of hip hop entertainer. I'm sure that's not part of the uniform."

Malik let out a shallow breath. *Who the hell this woman think she talkin' to?*

"I 'preciate the feedback, ma'am. You have yourself a nice evening." Malik gave her a nod and a small salute as he turned and reentered his truck. He looked over to make sure she still watched and turned the volume on his trap music louder. He gave her a wide smile, then nodded upward as he sped off.

Claudia slammed her door, frazzled by the man with her package. She was distracted throughout the rest of the meeting. At one point, Nick privately messaged her and asked if she needed anything or if she wanted company. She smiled at his thoughtfulness but declined. The only thing she wanted at the end of the meeting was food and a bottle of wine.

* * *

CLAUDIA HAD no earthly idea why she'd agreed to visit her parents' home this early in the afternoon—especially after such a long work week. Her Friday evening delivery drama from the night before had heightened her frustration, and she could barely settle herself down to sleep. Now she sat uncomfortably with a slight wine hangover.

Her twin sister, Victoria, sent a message in the family group chat that she had big news and wanted everyone at the house to hear it. She'd put everyone in capital letters. Claudia knew the emphasis was added for her. It wasn't that she didn't want to be there for her sister; it was that her sister rarely wanted Claudia around.

Claudia longed for the type of twin relationship where she already knew Victoria's news because she would've called her first. Weren't twins supposed to be close? She had more in common with her brother Winston Jr.—everyone in the family called him JW. Claudia recalled their youthful banter about how technically his name should be WJ, but he insisted JW sounded much cooler.

JW never got offended with Claudia's need for clarification. The memory about his nickname was a pleasant one, because they shared a laugh over it. If the same encounter had happened between the sisters, the results would have been catastrophic. Victoria wouldn't have been quite as gracious as JW. She would've elicited the support of her parents, while Claudia would be dumbfounded as to why she'd once again upset her.

Victoria hadn't arrived at the designated time. She made everyone wait like the thespian she was, so Claudia used the downtime to detail her gripes about her Glamazon debacle.

"Yo, what is that?" JW asked. He'd announced himself only after he'd read portions of Claudia's screen.

Claudia reached out and gave him a playful push. "Stop being nosy."

"What does having a grill have to do with delivering packages professionally? Did he throw the packages and break something? Did he steal them?"

"No."

"You're going to get this man fired if you send that." JW shook his head and threw a pillow at her, almost knocking her laptop to the ground.

"Claudia, you're the oldest. How can you still participate in this type of behavior?" Delores asked. She'd entered the dining area shortly after her only son.

Delores was Claudia's older, beautiful, and judgmental mother. Her crown was a luxurious gray and black color. She wore an off the side part with a press and whimsical spiral curls at the ends. Her wide leg pants flowed with her movements, as did the long sleeves of her cream chiffon top.

The Vaughn family was full of creatives. Delores and Claudia's father, Winston Sr. were the praise and worship ministers at their church. JW was the author and illustrator of a popular and lucrative comic book that went viral in several Asian countries, while her sister was a sought-after voice actor.

Claudia never felt like she measured up to their talent. It didn't matter how many promotions or pay increases she got—her family didn't understand why she wasted her time with corporate employment. She wished she could scream at the top of her lungs that the work she did was her version of creativity.

Claudia sighed and saved the email as a draft. "Sorry, Mama."

Her father shuffled into the room and threw an unenthusiastic greeting her way. "Hey, Claudy. I didn't think you'd make it with all those meetings you're always in."

Winston was a handsome silver fox. His hair was cut low, but his beard was what caught most people's attention. It had a full santa-esk texture. He kept himself in shape and had the speaking and singing voice of an angel.

Winston could easily date someone Claudia's age, if he kept his mouth shut. He had the judgmental bug like her mother. *I guess that's where I get it!*

"It's Saturday, Daddy. I generally don't take meetings over the weekend."

"You were pounding away on your computer a moment ago. I figured it must have been for work."

Before Claudia could respond, Victoria floated into the room dramatically like the family was her audience. She strutted in her stiletto sandals and threw her floor-length skirt to the side like she was on a runway.

"You've got to be kidding," Claudia muttered under her breath.

"Claudia, shhh. Your sister wants to share her news," Delores fussed.

Claudia's shoulders sagged, and her mouth fell open. She was a twenty-eight-year-old woman, but her family never ceased to make her feel like a petulant child. Victoria was like a mirror of what Claudia's life would be if her family embraced her.

They weren't identical, but they looked so much alike most people assumed they were. While Claudia was five feet seven, her sister was five feet three at best. They had the same texture of hair, with almost identical smiles. Claudia was a few shades lighter than Victoria and felt slightly envious of her sister's deep chocolate hue.

Victoria wore faux locs down her back, decorated with shells and jewelry that highlighted her beauty. She changed her hair more often than Claudia, who basically allowed her natural hair to do as it pleased. *Vicky's so pretty. I could never deny that, no matter how ugly her attitude is.*

"I've been cast as the wicked stepmother in the animated *Sleeping Dragon* movie," Victoria said with her hands high in the air.

Claudia cackled loudly. She couldn't contain herself. Of course, she was selected to play a villain. Victoria was evil, and she always had been. The family looked down on Claudia because they felt like her work wasn't important, but they expected her to fall over herself with praise because her sister would get paid money to be herself in a cartoon.

With tears of hysteria in her eyes, she managed to say, "Sorry, Vicky. That's great. Good for you."

"You're just mad my life is better than yours." Victoria propped her hands on her hips and glared at her twin.

"Let's not take it there. I've never been in competition with you."

"You're telling me you're not jealous of the attention I get from Mom and Dad?"

"Girls—" Winston started.

"I am. But we're not talking about Mom and Dad. We're talking about you insisting I'm here to hear about your success when you don't like me. Then you expect me to sing your high praises. Make it make sense, Vic."

"You're bitter."

Claudia stood. "Mom and Dad, I'm sorry I laughed at Vicky's news. But note that this is my attempt to walk away. I don't want to ruin her celebration, so I'm going to go."

"I think you should," was her mother's response.

Claudia's shoulders sank, and she released a frustrated breath of air. How the hell was this her family? If they didn't have such strong physical resemblances, Claudia would have sworn she was switched at birth.

"Claudy's all wound up because Tommy's wife is about to have baby number two," Victoria said as venom and ice dripped from both her words and the glare she held.

Claudia froze for long seconds as her sister's declaration washed over her. When she could no longer keep her cool, she charged in Victoria's direction. Unfortunately, JW was there to hold her back.

"It's not worth it," he coached. "She's not worth it."

Claudia allowed her brother to back her into the foyer attached to the dining area where she let out an audible groan of frustration.

"Why do you let her get to you like that?" he asked with genuine sincerity.

"Are you serious? Everyone in this family hates me. They treat me like I'm some kind of outsider. It's cruel because I get invited just to be left out."

"I know you don't wanna hear this, but Vicky's jealous of you." JW was cautious with his words.

"Boy, what?" Claudia re-entered the dining area with her little brother on her heels. "Don't worry. I'm just getting my things," Claudia announced as she packed her laptop into her designer bookbag. She avoided eye contact with her family, because the last thing she wanted was to feel shame for defending herself.

Victoria knew exactly what it would do to Claudia to hear her ex had another baby on the way.

Her hand was on the front door when her baby brother spoke up. "I don't hate you, Claudy. You're unorthodox, but so what. That's why she's jealous."

"This is juvenile. We're almost thirty—"

"When you're not here, all Mom and Dad talk about is you. They're worried about you working too much and concerned you might still be hung up over Tommy. It's cruel and unusual that they don't tell you to your face, but Vicky doesn't get half as much attention as you think she does."

Claudia shook her head, unable to grasp his point. She leaned in and gave him a hug.

"I love you too, WJ."

"I ain't say all that, and stop calling me WJ." He squirmed out of her grasp and pushed her away. He was four years younger than his sisters, but somehow more intuitive. "Yo, but for real. Don't get that black man fired. I'm serious."

"How do you know he's black?"

He stared at her, until they both broke into laughter. She said her goodbyes from the foyer and didn't wait for anyone other than her brother's response before she closed the door behind her.

Claudia left her parents' home deflated. Why did she continue to put herself in a position to feel bad about who she was?

She drove home determined to make the most of what remained of her afternoon. The work week was long, and she knew just the way to brighten her day.

She was barely out of her car before her hips swiveled in anticipation of her twerkout workout. Claudia may have been uptight in her real life, but when it came to dance, she let loose. It was exactly what she needed to escape from the heaviness of her situation.

Three

MALIK DECIDED he wouldn't save Thompson's deliveries until the end of his shift this time. The last encounter he had with Lady Butner about got him fired. He'd also been overly tired and hungry, and he had a good mind to shake the shit out of that woman until she learned better manners.

Like the hustler he was, he came up with a strategy for his most difficult customer. He'd estimated the best time for a Saturday delivery to Claudia would be after lunch, when he was still energized and just before his afternoon lull. As Malik rounded the street that featured her large estate, nestled in a cul-de-sac, he turned his music off. He would accommodate her until Thompson was back on his feet.

The package he had for her required a signature. Unfortunately, he wouldn't have the luxury of dropping it off without being seen. Malik sat in his seat and counted to ten. Maybe she'd see the Glamazon truck and meet him at the curb before he could step a ghetto sneaker to her lawn.

He chuckled to himself and exited his vehicle. Malik admired the architecture of her home. It reminded him of those homes designed by the famous white lady who cooked all the time but got locked up a few years back. He noticed Claudia Butner also had a talented landscaper. He was positive she hadn't put her hands to work.

He made it up her steps and to the front door without being noticed. Malik hoped she was gone for errands—maybe it was his lucky day. The muted sound of music squashed his hopes. Curiosity prompted him to look through the window before he rang her doorbell, and he was flabbergasted by what he saw.

A toned and usually high-strung Claudia was dressed in an all-black unnecessarily taunting yoga outfit. Malik hadn't forgotten how repulsed he'd been by her word choice by any means, but her body gave him a moment of amnesia.

The spandex pants were tight and hugged her ass nicely. The sports bra enhanced the shape of her titties, and if that wasn't enough to drive him wild, she wore a red-hot colored, long-sleeved hoodie that barely covered her bra.

With his jaw on the floor, Malik's libido increased when he heard Meg Thee Stallion say something about dropping her panties and her man smiling like they brought the food out. He was familiar with the song because it had made it on one of his upper body playlists.

Claudia held her body in the pushup position as she twerked up and down several times. Not only was it one of the sexiest things Malik had ever seen, but he knew firsthand how strong she must have been to do it. Her body was sculpted, but her ass moved freely like it had a mind of its own.

Convinced he'd seen enough, he decided to give Claudia another chance to speak to him like she had some sense. A woman with a body that beautiful could afford to have an off day as far as he was concerned.

Malik straightened his clothes and rubbed his hand across the back of his hair like he hadn't just brushed it in his truck less than ten minutes ago. Brushing his hair unnecessarily was another quirk he had that calmed him down. Only this time, he needed to calm the heated lust Claudia had stirred with her brazen dance moves.

He rang the doorbell with a charmed smile on his face. He wouldn't remove his grill for anybody, but he'd turned his music down like she'd demanded.

"What?" Claudia snatched the door open with an attitude. Her forehead was decorated with beads of sweat, and her clothes clung to her irresistible body.

How the hell somebody this fine act so horrendous? Malik blew out an exasperated breath. He reached into his pocket for a toothpick and took his time as he removed it from the plastic.

"I need your signature, Butner." His voice was even, but all the hope he had when he saw her glorious movement flew out the window when she opened her mouth.

"Can you please stop calling me Butner?"

Malik examined the package to ensure he had the correct name and address. "I was here last night. You're Claudia Vaughn Butner, right?"

"Butner is no longer my name," she said as she snatched the package from Malik's hands.

"Got it." Malik's facial expression was smug as he realized she wasn't a high falutin Butner; she was a bitter woman who hadn't gotten over her divorce to a Butner.

She signed for her package and all but threw his pen at him. He'd been as nice as he could, but he only had so much patience. Against his better judgment, he mumbled, "You'd think with all these pleasure packages I've delivered, you'd be a hell of a lot looser."

Claudia's eyes doubled in size. Before she could respond, he shrugged his large shoulders and turned on his heels. She could kiss his whole ass as far as he was concerned. She slammed her door, but he couldn't care less. Malik made it back to his truck, just in time to see there was another package assigned to her address.

"Fuck!"

The package didn't require a signature. Without a second thought, he exited the truck, walked back to the edge of her sidewalk, and tossed it on her lawn. *Bitch.*

Claudia heard the thud of what sounded like another delivery. She reopened the door to find the delivery man and truck gone, and her possession thrown onto the grass.

That was it! Claudia tried to listen to her brother's advice, but she had enough. Malik Malone would be off her route before the day was out. She'd done some digging on the Glamazon employee website after their first encounter and learned his full name. She hadn't taken to the internet to search anything about his personal life because that was of little interest to her.

What she wanted was a professional and quiet Glamazon employee to deliver her packages in peace. And Malik had the nerve to mention her intimate pleasure products—Claudia was mortified. He'd been tickled by his comment, and she never wanted to face him again.

He could deliver packages to the hood where baby mamas would love nothing more than to marvel at his slow gait and chiseled body. She could only imagine how they'd react to his charmed smile. *Ugh, he is seriously annoying.*

She sent the email she'd drafted after she included what happened this afternoon with the thrown package and rude remark. Claudia was certain she'd get his supervisor's attention when she added that she would take her business elsewhere. She hit send and slammed her laptop shut. One more day of the weekend, and she could return to her happy place—work, where things and people made sense.

* * *

MALIK'S SHIFT was over at last, but his work wasn't finished. Later tonight, he would reword a portion of his business plan since he'd attended a workshop for new clothing startups a few weeks ago. While he had a functional framework, his plan lacked elements germane to fashion.

He moseyed to his parents' front door and stretched his stiff body. He momentarily wondered if he'd gone too hard with his workout that morning. His mind drifted to thoughts of crazy ass, but undeniably fine Claudia Butner.

What the hell was that woman's problem? Malik had the right mind to toss her ass in her tidy, manicured bushes. He didn't get frazzled, but it was something about the way she spoke to him that set him off. He pulled out his phone and checked his money app. He was less than six months from his financial goal.

Malik decided on an amount that would give him twelve months of income to focus solely on Hood Body Briefs. He had no doubt that a year would be plenty of time to get his line in front of the right investors. He was willing to work twenty-hour days and fly to South Africa or Hong Kong if necessary. In order to attain the level of attention and flexibility his business required, he'd have to stay on with Glamazon until after Christmas. The Butners of the world would not stand in the way of his dreams, damn it.

Though he longed for a place to call his own, he cherished his time with his family. His parents' craftsman styled home felt reliable and secure. Malik needed the safety net while he went after his dreams. Their neighbors were all successful in their own right, and it was crucial for Malik to see folks who used their God-given gifts when he woke up and when he laid his head down to rest.

He'd barely turned the knob when John John, Malik's nephew, jumped from the couch like a tiny superhero. Malik never tired of how much the little four-year-old shared his face. John John resembled his uncle more than his father, and Malik made it a point to throw it in John's face whenever he stepped out of line with Markita. His sister was too good for him, but he wouldn't go there tonight. He'd endured enough stress for a month on his last shift.

"I know for a fact you're supposed to be asleep," Malik said and bit out something that was a mixture of a laugh and cough. John John had jumped into his arms with his baby blanket tied around his neck like a makeshift cape.

"Hero hero's work at night. Like you, Uncle Mayeek."

Malik lifted him above his head and walked him around the living room to give him the full experience of flight.

"I know you didn't," Markita fussed from the door. Her voice sounded heavy like she'd carried the weight of the world in her small frame. If John John was the little boy version of Malik, Markita was the female version. "He was in bed thirty minutes ago," she added.

"It's OK. I'll take him. You rest yourself."

Markita kissed her teeth and gave John John a playful pat to his butt.

"Goodnight, Mommmmmy," he sang as his uncle Malik carried him high in the air toward Markita's room.

Fifteen long minutes later, Malik reemerged.

"Made you read him a bedtime story, didn't he?" his sister asked with a smirk on her ebony-colored face.

Malik nodded and stretched his neck.

"He played you, because he already had me and Daddy read him several books."

The twins laughed at Markita's only child.

"What's up with you? I can tell you've been crying." Malik took a seat on the sofa opposite his sister and extended his long legs.

"Same old, same old. You just got off work. I'm sure the last thing you want is to hear my drama."

"John fuckin' up again?" Malik scooted to the edge of his seat, ready to handle his nephew's father. He had zero respect for the way he treated Markita. Even if he wasn't related to her, Malik couldn't comprehend how a man could treat the mother of his children like trash. It was the most ass backwards shit he'd ever heard.

"I caught him with Ava." Markita fiddled with the edge of a pillow as she shared the story with Malik.

Pretty was an understatement when it came to his sister's appearance. She was objectively stunning. They had the pictures to prove it. When she was a baby, and later as a young child, strangers approached them and offered to pay their mother to take her picture with the intent to paste them on advertisements.

When Malik was about ten, he asked his parents if he was ugly, because people never asked him to model. The family made it a running joke that he wasn't quite pretty enough.

Things got worse when they entered grade school. He stayed in fights over Markita. His dad had to explain to him that other boys found her attractive. After he stopped laughing, Malik realized while he was understandably unable to perceive his sister as good looking, boys were interested in her and had been ever since. John was jealous; it was simple, and it was obvious.

Malik's jaw clenched. "What did he say?"

"He said I wasn't supposed to be back home. After he dismissed her, he commenced to tell me I needed to leave if I was going to cry all night."

"The fuck?" Malik stood with his arms flexed. It was about time he reminded John who the fuck he dealt with. Malik wasn't about *that* life. He didn't carry his weapon around to handle verbal disputes or misunderstandings that could be solved with his fists, but John had taken things too far.

"He sent you and John John away tonight?"

Markita nodded. Then, in an accent that mirrored his, said, "Leave it alone."

"What?" Malik paced the carpet to keep himself calm.

"I don't want you involved. He's John John's dad."

Malik cracked his knuckles and stretched his body. He'd been tense and on edge since his run in with the Butner chick, and John's antics didn't help. Malik secretly wondered if he'd gotten his sister pregnant on purpose to lock her down.

Once again, John was an idiot, because Markita's popularity with men only increased once she had her son and her body got thicker. Shit was annoying as hell for Malik, and apparently for John.

Malik yawned and slurred an annoyed, "Aight. But I promise you, your boy's all out of passes." He scratched his face above his eyebrow and moved to leave the room.

"Time to go to work with your draws?" Markita laughed lightly, but Malik still saw pain in her eyes. He'd let it ride for now, but he'd meant what he said.

"You say that now. My draws gon' take you and our whole family to one of them five thousand square feet homes."

"I can't wait."

Malik headed to his room to remove his brightly colored work garments. He'd take a quick shower and handle Hood Body Briefs work at his desk for at least three hours before he'd call it a night. The days were long, but he was focused. He didn't have any evidence yet, but he could feel he was close to something magical.

Four

WITH HER EMAIL sent and her workout complete, the reality of Claudia's situation closed in on her. Another Saturday evening had come, and she was alone. She was always alone. Against her better judgment, she poured a glass of wine and curled up with her personal laptop. She knew it wasn't a good idea to check social media when no one else was around to intervene or interrupt.

She replayed Victoria's words repeatedly in the deep recesses of her mind. Tommy was about to have another baby. Her eyes stung along with the welcomed sensation of the wine she gulped down like water.

Claudia had a burner account that she used to stalk social media profiles. She originally created it because she felt like Victoria had restrictions on what Claudia could see. She was right.

The pain of that reality was short lived. There were stories and images of Vicky's first dates and trips Claudia hadn't known about. Everything Victoria posted with the intention of hiding was inconsequential as far as Claudia was concerned. But she'd gone down a rabbit hole when she saw a comment from Tommy on Vicky's page.

He'd referred to her as his favorite Vaughn sister. When Claudia read those simple words, she'd been devastated. She made the mistake of clicking on his profile, and the images of his perfect, happy family knocked the wind out of her.

Tommy's new wife didn't work. She was a stay-at-home wife and mother. From the pictures, she seemed to be the opposite of who Claudia was at her core.

Claudia hadn't always worked at her current level of intensity, but she loved what she did. She couldn't imagine not having some type of job. Wife number two looked like she was created for the fully domesticated role.

Her first pregnancy was highlighted in ten-second videos with painfully adorable music. A video of the two of them at a birthing center went viral, when their child was born without so much as a sneeze from his wife.

She was pregnant again. Claudia sat on her cozy chaise lounge and opened the page again. She tormented herself with the curated content of how his wife revealed the pregnancy to Tommy. She had their oldest child give Tommy the pregnancy stick. What bothered Claudia the most was the way he gazed at his second wife. He'd looked at Claudia the same way up until she shared his last name. Then he seemed to simply tolerate her.

Picture after picture of smiling, flawless faces did a number on Claudia's self-esteem. If she had any self-control, she would have signed off an hour ago. She found herself past Tommy's page, to the wife's page, then on the wife's parents' pages. She had a close relationship with them, and it seemed that Tommy did as well. Claudia was in a downward spiral of comparison.

Her parents cringed whenever Claudia wanted to embrace them or take pictures of any kind. Most of her family pictures were of her and JW, or with her halfway out of the image.

Claudia's vulnerable and tipsy state transported her thoughts back two years ago when she was approached by Tommy's mistress.

Claudia's day started great, although she and Tommy seemed to be in a two-week silent fight. She never wanted to upset him, so even though he'd treated her differently, she refused to confront him about it.

Tommy had been the one to pursue her in college and had done all he could to convince her they should be together as a married couple. She told her mom how things had shifted, but her mother assured her it was simply a seven-year itch, and it would eventually pass.

Claudia pointed out that they hadn't been married seven years yet but was hushed and accused of looking for trouble. She eventually dropped it. That day, she planned to do a little work at her favorite cafe.

The place was hip and full of the creative energy Claudia wished she had. Her work couldn't be farther from that of the other patrons who discussed new startups and took international calls—Claudia dealt in products and accessibility—but she loved the environment, nonetheless.

It used to be both Tommy and Claudia's favorite place, but lately, he showed little interest. She pushed thoughts of her marriage aside and ordered a coffee and coffee cake. Her butt had barely hit the seat when a breathtakingly beautiful woman with a rounded belly approached her.

Claudia stood. "You can sit here if it's more comfortable."

"I'll stand. I came to speak with you," the woman said and propped her hand on her hip.

"Do I know you?" She looked faintly familiar. Claudia recognized her from the cafe but couldn't recall having spoken to her.

"No. But I know Tom."

Claudia sat back down. She could now hear irritation in the woman's voice. "Who is Tom?"

"Thomas Butner."

Claudia's stomach lurched. Tommy had refused to ever go by the name on his birth certificate. But it was clear she knew him personally.

"How do you know my husband?" Claudia asked. Though the answer was obvious to her and a few nearby customers who did their best to act like they couldn't hear.

"We're together. He's just afraid to leave you. But I'm halfway through this pregnancy, and it's not fair to me to wait around for you to take a hint."

Claudia stood and circled the table.

"You better be glad you're pregnant; otherwise, I'd beat the shit out of you. You have some nerve talking about my marriage as if it's inconvenience for you and your plans."

The woman laughed in her face. Claudia's expression was even, but on the inside, she felt like the town idiot. How long had he been cheating?

How long would he have waited to come clean if his mistress hadn't approached her? Fucking Coward!

Claudia gathered her things as she felt fury rise in her belly and tears well in her eyes.

"That's right, leave. And clear out of my house quickly."

Claudia turned to face her. The cafe was eerily quiet as everyone looked on. She certainly couldn't justify fighting a pregnant woman.

Claudia scanned the area and said to no one in particular, "Her damn face ain't pregnant." She reached back and slapped the mess out of the woman. She heard 'ohs' and 'ahhs' on her way out, but no one intervened—not even to see if the other woman was OK. Serves her right.

Claudia left the cafe broken. The woman didn't care that she'd just blown up Claudia's world; she had Tommy and his money to hold her close.

Claudia never returned to the home she built and decorated with Tommy. Shortly before the birth of their first child, they were publicly engaged. And as soon as his divorce from Claudia was final, he married his mistress.

Tears streamed her face as she berated herself for how she'd spent the evening.

The clock said it was well past midnight. Maybe she could sleep in on Sunday and skip to the work week where she felt accepted. It was where she belonged.

* * *

MALIK BOPPED into the hub of Glamazon on Monday, fifteen minutes early. He'd done his morning ritual of a run, a workout, and listened to a few chapters of Taylor Dawn's new audiobook. It was like his morning coffee.

Because he picked up a few additional shifts, he'd moved his retirement date up. At the rate he went, he could leave his delivery job before the holidays.

"Malone, in my office," Hal said. He still hadn't moved his wide ass from that worn chair, and Malik wondered if he propped himself up and slept there.

"Top of the morning to you too, Hal." Malik took his time as he entered the glass encased office. He was uncomfortable, as other employees passed by speculating what the meeting was about. "Everything good?"

"Have a seat," Hal responded.

Malik huffed but sat in an old chair with his back to his coworkers. *What the hell is this about?*

"Customer satisfaction is our number one priority. You're aware of this, right?"

Malik looked at him as if he needed Hal to get to the got damn point.

"I don't care what you wear in your mouth. That's between you and your dentist. I couldn't care less about the music you listen to or how loud you choose to listen. That's between you and the person who'll inevitably sell you a hearing aid."

"Are you going somewhere with this, boss? Or you invited me in here to criticize my lifestyle choices to my face?"

"Very funny. My point is, I don't care. But if a customer wants you to gently lay their packages two inches to the left of their front door, I need my guys to do as the customers wish. Don't be a hero and stack them at the right."

"Huh?"

"I got an email this weekend from one of Thompson's stops. Claudia Vaughn Butner."

Holy shit!

"Yes. She described you to a T. Said you were unprofessional in the way you addressed her and in how you spoke about the nature of her personal packages. She also said you threw one of them."

"OK, look, Hal—"

"No, Malone. You look. I can't have complaints like these, let alone someone as connected as a Butner. She threatened to take her business somewhere other than Glamazon."

"What are you saying?" Malik's jaw clenched, and he prayed Hal wouldn't overlook all the backbreaking extra hours and deliveries he'd done because of one miserable customer.

"I have to let you go. I'm sorry."

* * *

TO CLAUDIA'S DELIGHT, the weekend was officially over. She never understood why people hated Mondays. It was when she was the freshest. She woke without the aid of her alarm clock and slipped on the workout clothes she laid out the night before.

While she walked, she reflected on how she wanted a full life, even if there was no one there to live it with her. Other than work and her brother, all she had in the world was her pet snake, Red.

Claudia got the snake when she'd learned about Tommy's first baby. She'd gone to the pet store convinced she needed a dog in her life to love her unconditionally. But as the owner went on and on about how much attention a puppy required, her eyes glazed over. She pointed to the snake, and after a few instructions on the appropriate temperature, shedding, and how to feed the snake and clean the tank, she was good to go.

Claudia let her mind wander about how her snake's black, yellow, and, of course, red scales attracted her. Red never had any issues, and she never tried to bite her. She was always a listening ear. They had an understanding. It helped that Red was nonvenomous. Claudia could also take a trip for up to a week, and her snake would be fine unattended.

The morning breeze kissed Claudia's face, and she smiled brightly. She loved her neighborhood and how her neighbors took pride in the way in which they maintained the aesthetics. Today would be a good day; she could feel it.

Claudia returned home from her brisk walk and sang in the shower with a new surge of endorphins. It was six thirty when she finished her after-shower routine. She would allow the body oils to set while she made her smoothie, dressed in her favorite robe.

The sound of rapid, percussive pounds to the front door startled her and made her drop her smoothie. It spilled across her marble floor and ruined the freshly cleaned area.

Steam radiated from her ears as she stomped toward the source of contention without concern for her wardrobe or who might be respon-sible for the incessant knocks.

"What?" she yelled. Claudia's robe wasn't fastened, and her natural hair splayed in every direction. But her appearance was the last thing on her mind. Whoever invaded her solace and caused her to spill her drink would have hell to pay.

She was met with a pair of hickory-colored eyes filled with a similar fury. She almost didn't recognize Malik in plain clothes. *Damn!* Her eyes unintentionally raked over his hard body. She could see his muscles bulged through his shirt and jeans.

It was almost as if he'd gone through a Clark Kent type of transformation. Without the blinding canary yellow clothing, she could appreciate the hair that traveled his jawline and joined at the apex of the chin he rubbed from time to time. His mouth parted slightly, and the diamonds inside taunted her with what she knew could be a good time.

Malik Malone was fine, and Claudia wasn't sure how she'd been able to ignore it so easily before. He was wider than what she was used to, but she could adjust. Unashamed of where her thoughts had gone, her gaze unintentionally fell to the area between his legs. *Get a hold of yourself, girl!*

"What the hell is your problem, Butner?" Malik growled. He was pissed, but still hadn't rushed his words—his southern accent never left him.

She pulled her robe closed, suddenly aware of her nakedness. "I could ask you the same damn thing. Why are you—"

"You bitch!" Malik didn't make it a habit of calling women anything other than what their mothers named them, but Claudia had gone too damn far. He snatched the toothpick from his mouth because that shit hadn't helped calm his nerves at all. "You got me fired because I played my music loud and because I wear a grill that most likely fuels all those nighttime pleasure sessions you havin'." He grinned at the insult he threw her way, but the taunting expression on his lips didn't match the rage in his eyes.

I got him fired?

As if Malik could hear her naive thought process, he continued. "What did you think would happen, Ms. Butner?" He'd put an emphasis on Ms. because he knew it was a sore spot for her. He didn't give a shit because he was pissed.

Her little stunt would delay his financial plan to focus on his business full time. "You sent a long ass email to my boss, threatening to take your business elsewhere. Do you see any other way this could have possibly played out?"

Claudia was speechless. She hadn't intended to get him fired. She could hear JW's voice in her head, and she wished she'd listened. She wanted Malik off her route, but she hadn't wanted him without a job.

"I thought you'd get taken off my route," she said, much quieter than she normally spoke.

"Bullshit. I call bullshit! You think your name alone isn't a flex? Like that shit don't hold weight?"

She hadn't thought about it. Claudia had tried unsuccessfully to scrub her married name from her mail and her important documents, but it seemed to follow her around like bad credit.

She attempted to say something, though she wasn't sure anything she wanted to say would help. But he kept on before she had a chance.

"Claudia Vaughn Butner, you are a self-righteous, mean spirited, icy, and lonely shell of a woman." He turned his back before he shook the shit out of her like he wanted. Malik had never laid a hand on a woman, but he didn't trust himself with Claudia. "You need some dick," he said over his shoulder.

Mortified once again, Claudia slammed the door. Only this time, she wasn't enraged; she was embarrassed and overcome with despair. Malik's words stung much worse than his comment about her pleasure products. He'd called her a shell of a woman. Tears streamed her face, and she released audible wails. She'd finally met a Monday she didn't love.

* * *

MALIK FOUND himself with a new gig by hump day. There was no way he would let a bitter bitch steal his joy. He had shit to do, so he replaced his Glamazon position with an equally shoddy but lucrative company for a go-getter like himself.

Postbuddies was not how he envisioned spending his hours during the day. Customers and food were much different than customers and packages. For one, the smell of the product clung to his clothes. He'd been astounded to find the new employer he delivered for had a similar delivery truck as Glamazon.

It made no sense to Malik how they expected to efficiently and appropriately transport someone's food in a truck designed to deliver safely wrapped packages. If it were his company, it would be mandatory to transport food in cars and SUVs. But this wasn't his company.

Malik's thoughts were interrupted by the weather forecast prediction of another one of Georgia's monstrous thunderstorms. With that, he turned off his app and decided to head home for the night. He'd made a good deal of money, and with the way some of the customers tipped, Butner may have moved his retirement date up.

His smile widened, though her name put a bad taste in his mouth. The route to his parents' home was mostly dark. He'd memorized the twists and turns and felt comfortable with the truck despite the rain that fell. The radio was late with this one, because the night went from quiet to a torrential downpour within minutes.

Malik wasn't far from his house when he noticed a woman and her car dangerously close to oncoming traffic. *Where are her flares or her hazard lights? This woman is about to get herself killed. Damn, her body is nice.*

Malik slowed his vehicle and pulled alongside her once he turned his hazards on. *I'll be got damned. Claudia Butner?*

"It's not safe for you to be next to your car this close to the road!" Malik yelled over the boisterous sound of the rain. His hand scratched the area below his hairline double-time.

"It's not working! If I could move it, I wouldn't be standing in the rain like a jackass." She rolled her eyes at him like he was the inconvenience.

Malik shook his head and pulled off. Unbothered that a bit of the splash from his tires added to her already soaked clothing. *Fuck that bitch!* He'd gotten less than a few yards before he could hear his sister's nagging ass voice. He shook it off and kept driving. Then he heard his mother in his head. She would kick his ass if she knew he'd left a woman in the rain on a dark road.

He was uncomfortable but able to push through until he wondered what his grandmother, Cicely, would think. She would be disappointed. *Shit!*

Malik made a U-turn and pulled up beside Claudia's car once again. "Get in."

"Why would I want to get in your—" She yelled until he cut her off.

"It's not safe, woman, damn! Get your shit and get in with your difficult ass."

She stomped. Malik shook his head in disbelief at her childish behavior. What the hell did she think he would do? He smirked when she slipped on her way to the passenger side of her car. Claudia grabbed her bag and quickly shuffled to Malik's delivery truck.

A car as expensive as the one Claudia owned shouldn't have broken down on her the way it did. He wondered if she'd forgotten to fill it with gas. The passenger side chair sloshed when Claudia took a seat. He took in her disheveled look and did his best to hold in his laughter.

She turned and glared at him. Malik didn't break eye contact. Besides, he wasn't responsible for her wet clothes or her stranded vehicle. This was her karma, and he was quite tickled with the sudden turn of events.

He cautiously pulled his truck back onto the road as a fierce clap of thunder ripped through the sky, almost simultaneously with a bright flash of light.

"The storm is close. We better get off this road."

"Take me home!"

Malik shook his head again. Couldn't the damn woman hear? They were in danger if they continued on their current route. Couldn't she see? There was no way she missed the sight of lightning and the increased downpour of rain.

Malik continued toward Claudia Butner's half-million-dollar estate. Out of the corner of his eye, he noted her tremble because of her dampened clothes and the unforgiving wind. Malik's vehicle didn't have doors on the side, and the more they drove, the more Claudia shivered.

He also didn't miss the thick ringlets of her natural hair. They hung around her head like a halo. She looked innocent with her hair that way. He reached behind him toward the back seat.

"What are you doing? Focus on the road!" she shouted. He

wondered if she was always this bitchy or if maybe she was afraid of the storm and that caused her to kick it up a notch.

He retrieved what he'd extended his long arm for, and a hush settled over her endless complaints. Malik tossed her one of his hooded sweatshirts. She held it for long moments before she finally had the good sense to thank him.

"Thank you."

"I'm sorry, what!" he yelled. His voice taunted her, and she fought back a smile.

"I said *thank you*!" She lifted the all-black hoodie over her head and inhaled his masculine scent. Malik's essence and a bit of his cologne clung to the shirt and embraced Claudia's body like a warm hug. Her shivers ceased and she relaxed, as much as possible, against the back of the seat.

"What's a hood body brief?" she asked.

Malik continued to weave the vehicle through darkened roads, illuminated only by the momentary flashes of lightning. He gazed over at her and then back at the road.

"Is this some sort of gang?" Claudia smirked like she was pleased with herself and nearly flew forward when he slammed on the brakes.

"Shut up."

"Excuse me?" Claudia couldn't believe the way he'd spoken to her. He needed to get her home before the storm got worse.

"You're in *my* ride. You broke down, remember? I'm taking you home because my Yaya would kick my ass if I left you unprotected and in the dark the way you were."

"What's a Ya—" Her voice was mocking like he hadn't spoken a word of English.

"My grandmother. Everything you say to me drips with judgment and entitlement."

She opened her mouth to speak, but slow paced or not, Malik wasn't finished.

"Who hurt you?" He glared at her, and she could practically feel the steam coming from him.

She opened her mouth again, then closed it. What the hell was she supposed to say? Being a bitch was her defense mechanism. It was the only thing that protected her from a nervous breakdown after her divorce, and the only way she'd survived her family. But this wasn't a therapy session. Bump him!

"It must be a gang," she mumbled.

"Fuck you. It's not a gang. For your information, Hood Body Briefs is the name for my clothing line."

Claudia chuckled.

"The clothing line I intend to focus one hundred percent of my energy toward once I've saved a year's income. A goal you delayed when you got me fired, Ms. Butner." Malik's chest heaved with anger. "You know what? I don't have to explain myself to you."

He pulled his car off to the side of the road, splashing pockets of water when he did. Once his car was safely in park, he unbuckled his seat belt and stood.

"Get out."

"What?" Claudia unbuckled her seat belt, too, but she had no intention of leaving his truck until he took her home. She scowled at him.

"I said get your ungrateful, nasty ass attitude out." He seethed as he stared down at her. No one had ever gotten him worked up the way Claudia did. His chest visibly rose and fell as she frowned back up at him.

"No!"

He closed the distance between them and grabbed her by the arm. Claudia's breath caught. The rain continued to beat against the roof of the truck, but the air shifted between the two of them.

Malik pulled her closer and studied her hazelnut features. She'd gotten under his skin, and now all his body wanted was to kiss the scowl off her pouty lips. So, he did.

Claudia returned the kiss with equal passion fueled by her pent-up sexual frustration. His rough hands found the back of her head, and she melted into him. Before she could prepare herself, he'd lifted her and turned toward the back of the truck. He moved his mouth from hers to watch his step, and she took the opportunity to latch onto his neck.

Malik groaned in pleasure. She sucked his neck like he was a steak dinner, and she was a starved woman. Claudia hadn't been with a man in much too long to remember. But the few moments in Malik's arms felt like it more than made up for the time she'd missed. He kicked aside the clutter on the floor and gently returned her to her feet.

She stared at him, unsure of what would happen next, but certain she didn't want whatever it was to stop. He pulled his arctic-blue uniform over his head, and the sight of his bare chest made Claudia's center thump. She was wetter than the rain that fell outside of the truck.

"Take this shit off, Claudia."

Claudia pulled his hoodie over her head like she was on autopilot. She peeled the wet blouse off her damp skin and shimmied out of her skirt.

"Hurry up."

She'd removed her clothing, with the exception of her bra and thigh-high panty hose and garter belt. It was hard for her to concentrate when his gaze was on her the way it was. His angry face and his lust filled one were practically the same. His eyes surveyed her, and though he'd commanded her to hurry up, everything about him still moved at the pace of a southern man with all the time in the world.

He lowered, and Claudia thought she'd choke on her own spit. Malik was a lot of things, but weak he was not. As he settled on his knees in front of her, he'd never looked so powerful. She was waxed and had paired her garter set with a sheer thong, but the fact that she knew she looked hot didn't stop her from wanting to fidget.

He peered up at her, and through gritted teeth, he said, "Didn't I say take this shit off?"

Before she could respond, he reached out and ripped the lingerie off her. Claudia almost orgasmed from sheer excitement. If he could elicit those feelings without having touched her, she was overwhelmed with what would happen when he did.

A moan escaped her mouth, and a smile covered his. She took in the infamous grill she'd criticized before. The diamond fangs outlined his canine teeth, while the bottom row was capped. They seemed to twinkle against his sparkling white teeth. *Damn!*

"You want me?"

Claudia looked away. Why the hell was he talking? Wasn't he supposed to get right to it? She was practically naked. She fidgeted under his admiration. She'd never been looked at in this way. And she'd certainly never had a man wait for verbal consent. What the hell was this?

"If you want me to do what needs to be done, I need to hear you say it. Tell me you want me, Claudia. I won't touch you until you do."

A river pooled between her legs, and she shifted, uncomfortable with the level of desire and anticipation that happened inside her body. While he waited, Malik placed his nose next to her treasure and took a deep breath in. "Damn!"

"OK, yes." She rolled her eyes.

Malik chuckled. "I'mma need you to tell me, baby. Otherwise, you're gonna have to stay pent up."

"I want you, Malik. I want you so fucking bad it hurts."

He looked up at her like her words unlocked a magical savage. Malik effortlessly lifted her from his kneeled position. Claudia didn't think it was possible, so she was caught off guard, and a small yelp escaped her lips. He placed her legs around his waist, and her head fell back the moment she felt the stiffness between his legs. She just knew it would be good.

Thunder clapped outside, but neither of them seemed concerned. He captured her bottom lip in his mouth and bit it gently. He kissed her and settled her on his lap, and rested so he sat down on his knees. Malik continued to move at his painfully methodical pace, yet Claudia didn't feel he'd gone too slow.

He tugged at her bra, which was conveniently clasped in the front. Malik moved one hand to her ass and the other to the middle of her back. His mouth found the nipple of her left breast, and Claudia couldn't quiet the moan that escaped her lips. She threw her head back again and rocked against him. She wanted him inside of her right now.

He gently moved her from his lap as he lifted to remove his uniform pants. When Claudia saw the bulge between Malik's legs, her mouth watered.

"Are... are these them?" she asked incoherently.

"What?" Malik chuckled, as if it was perfectly normal for her to lose her good sense while she stared between his legs.

"The hood body briefs?" She swallowed loudly and allowed her eyes to meet his.

He nodded.

"Damn."

He removed the underwear, he was sure would make him millions, fully aware he had an audience of one. He watched as her throat bobbed when she saw him fully naked. Malik moved to find his wallet to get protection, and Claudia was unashamed at the way her eyes escorted his muscular ass around the vehicle. She wanted him, and she wanted him badly.

He sheathed himself and knelt before her. He used his hoodie and laid it down, but he had no doubt the punishment he'd give her would have her sore for days to come.

"Hurry up," Claudia pleaded.

Malik wore a grin as he grabbed the sides of her thighs and pulled her forcefully toward him. He used his hand to feel between her legs and contorted his face when he realized just how ready she was. Claudia tried to lay back, but Malik wasn't having it.

"Nah, fuck that. Stand up."

Claudia looked surprised, but she did what he asked.

"You want me to hurry up? Let's go." He lifted and pushed her body against the wall of the truck. He grabbed her hips tightly and entered her in one swift motion.

Claudia moaned loudly.

"I think I need to do something about that damn mouth of yours."

"Yes, daddy."

"You fuckin' right. I'm the daddy now." Malik slapped her ass, and before he'd gotten more than a few strokes, her legs shook.

"Shit!" She cried.

Malik plowed inside of her time and time again, and Claudia sang her praises loudly.

"You gonna watch the way you talk to me?"

Claudia nodded, but that wasn't good enough. Malik stilled. She craned her head to see what the holdup was. Rain and thunder continued to serenade them like a vibrant background music.

"I asked you a question, Claudia. And I'm not gonna fuck you until you agree."

"Please," she begged. She wanted his masterpiece of a dick to continue the punishment it gave her. She felt like she'd die if he didn't finish.

"Please? Hell no. Not until you tell me you gonna stop talking to me like you crazy."

She nodded again, and Malik flexed the muscle inside of her, making his dick bounce. Her eyes closed, and her mouth fell open.

"Yes," she whined.

"Yes, what?" He slammed into her again, then stilled.

"I'm gonna talk to you better, daddy. Just please don't stop."

Malik grabbed the back of her neck and continued his sensuous punishment. When Claudia came, she was sure she saw stars. She'd never tried drugs, but she couldn't be convinced she hadn't left her body and floated above the truck to watch the rest of the Malik pussy annihilator show.

Malik was pleased at how well she took his dick, but he was nowhere near finished with her. He wanted to see how far he could push her toned legs back, and he'd need to be on top of her to put it to the test.

"Lay down, Claudia." The deep timber of his voice made her head swim. To think she almost missed out on this had her twisted in knots.

She lay down, and he paused to take her in. The dark brown skin that covered Claudia's body was velvety smooth. When she wasn't spitting venom at him, she was achingly attractive.

"Damn, girl."

Now Claudia grinned. He'd been so upset with her earlier. She had no idea the amount of sexual tension between them until they'd kissed.

He used his large hands and stroked the inside of her thighs. She'd already gotten her pleasure; why was he still pleasing her? She shifted under his touch and his gaze.

"Am I going too slow for you, Ms. Vaughn?" His words came out as measured as they always did. His accent irritated her when they'd met, but now it had her on the verge of another orgasm.

She nodded because she couldn't speak when he looked at her like she was a meal.

He settled between her legs and lifted them to his waist. She felt him pulse against her split, and it only increased her desire to feel him back inside of her.

"Please," she whined.

Malik's eyebrows were bunched together like he was in pain. "Your naggin' ass voice bugged the shit out of me before. But now," he closed his eyes for a brief moment, "I almost came when you said please."

He entered her swiftly, and Claudia moaned her appreciation. He lifted her legs and rested the back of them on his shoulders.

"Yes," she moaned. Malik used his hand to cover her mouth. Another sensual moan like that and he'd be done. He could feel her smirk beneath his hands.

"You like when I'm frazzled, Claudia?"

She nodded. He still had his hand across her mouth. He entered her repeatedly, at a painfully slow pace. Claudia wanted him to plow into her. He tormented her with his measured strokes, and she had had enough. She licked his hand, and his eyebrows bunched again. He kept his hand in place, so she continued to use her tongue to stroke his rough hand.

He removed it and went to work just as she hoped. He fucked her until she was sure she'd have rug burns on her back. Her legs shook, and she experienced another human-induced orgasm. Those toys didn't have shit on Malik Malone.

Claudia's body ached, though she experienced immense pleasure. He'd been inside of her for what felt like an hour, until she turned her head and clamped down on his earlobe. Her yoni followed suit when she tightened around his dick with a fierce Kegel—It was his undoing. He roared her name and collapsed on top of her. She accepted his weight, and immediately fell into a deep satiated sleep.

Five

CLAUDIA'S EYES OPENED. She was disoriented and unsure where she was. There was total darkness in every direction, but she didn't panic since she could still feel and smell him. Her nipples hardened at the memory of what they'd done.

His light snores alerted her that Malik had fallen asleep as well. She was still naked but found his Postbuddies uniform draped over her along with his heavy arm. What time was it? She gently held up her arm to awaken her watch and saw that it was two a.m.

The storm had stopped, and the noise from it was replaced with the unfamiliar sounds of wildlife. What if something climbed into his truck? What if somebody robbed them?

"I stay strapped," Malik said in a voice full of sex and sleep. It was as if he could feel her almost panic. *Damn this man is sexy!*

"Excuse me?"

"You heard me."

"You have a gun in here?" she asked in an accusatory tone.

Malik lifted his head. "Do I need to remind you what you promised just a few hours ago?"

She smirked, but even in the dark, she could feel he was serious.

"Are you allowed to carry a weapon?" she amended.

He nodded.

"OK, good."

He attempted to remove his arm and gather himself, but Claudia pulled him back to her.

"Not yet," she pleaded.

Malik adjusted himself closer to where her body laid. She cuddled up with him and fell back asleep.

* * *

THIS TIME when her eyes popped open, he was upright and had pulled on those intoxicating briefs. She squinted in the dark as he moved around, dressing himself in everything but the shirt she had over her naked body. She was cold without the comfort of his body heat.

"I shouldn't have you out here like this. This shit ain't safe." Malik seemed disappointed in himself when he switched on the overhead light. Claudia saw random boxes, tape, and the typical delivery equipment alongside where she was seated. She'd had the best sex of her life in the back of a truck.

"I enjoyed myself."

He grinned. "Claudia Vaughn Bu—"

"Don't say that name, please. I don't want to ruin the end of whatever this is by becoming a bitch."

"Fair enough. Claudia Vaughn, what do you enjoy about me?"

She fought not to roll her eyes and shifted under his flirtatious gaze. "Uh, I absolutely enjoyed those briefs." The smirk she wore was sincere, but she hadn't spent enough time with Malik for him to accept it.

"Fuck. Is the only time you're not busting my balls is when I'm inside you?"

Claudia burst into laughter, covering her mouth as she continued. Malik snagged his Postbuddies shirt and grimaced when he saw her bare breasts. Even as he believed she poked fun at him, his body responded to the sight of hers. She stood and approached him, but he held out his hands.

"It's not gonna work this time. You can't keep talking down to me and think because you're sexy, I'll forget."

Claudia came as close to Malik as she could without touching him.

"I'm being sincere. I know I'm a bitch at times..."

"Most times," he added.

"I deserve that. But I mean it. I'm not laughing at your idea. I was laughing at your comment about busting your balls. I thought your vision was brilliant when you first mentioned it. Then I saw them. Those briefs will be widespread in no time. I'll be surprised if it takes three months."

Malik regarded her, unsure of if she'd meant what she said.

"I work with a lot of people who would love to buy into a company like yours." She absently picked up his hooded sweatshirt and covered herself. A small smile played across his face at the ease in which she'd done it. "Let me set something up with an investor I know."

Malik stilled. "Nah, I'm good." He didn't like where the conversation was headed.

"But—"

"I don't need your handouts," he bit out in frustration.

"It's the least I can do for getting you fired."

Malik scratched the space between his hairline and his eyebrow. "I'm gonna take you home before we start fighting again."

"What did I say?"

"Just drop it." He leaned down and kissed the pout on her lips. Claudia decided maybe it was a good idea to let it go, though she was clueless as to how she'd offended him this time.

She gathered her damp clothing from a pile in the back of the truck. Claudia was naked with the exception of Malik's hoodie. He strapped himself in the driver's seat but found it difficult to focus on the road with the way her legs looked when they were unobstructed from the panty hose and skirt she'd worn a few hours ago. When he lifted his eyes from her body, he found she was in deep contemplation.

He wanted to ask more about her. He wondered if they'd link up again but felt it best not to push his luck. Although the rain had stopped completely, the night sky was still void of light. They arrived in Claudia's division in no time. He pulled the truck in front of her house and cut the engine off without saying a word.

With a long sigh, she said, "Thank you, Malik."

"Not a problem."

He was distant, and she could tell. Claudia wasn't hung up with whether she saw him again or not, but she felt it important that he knew she meant what she'd said.

"I'm serious." She unstrapped herself and positioned her body in his direction. Malik's eyes bounced between her legs and her flawless face. "I'm sorry for getting you fired and throwing you off your deadline with your business. It's a profitable one, or it will be soon, and I'm not just saying that because of what you just did to me." She blushed when her eyes fluttered toward the back of his truck.

"I can't wait to see your billboard." She stood with her heels in her hand. "You should demand they let you be the model. Every girl will want her man to wear them, and every guy will want to look like you in them."

She descended the stairs of his vehicle and turned back to throw him a wave. He returned her wave with a gradual upward nod. He allowed her words to dance in his head and wondered if she was capable of being genuine. Claudia ambled to her door and told him to go ahead.

"I'll wait until you get inside. Wouldn't be right if I left a second sooner," he called out to her.

For Claudia to have lived in the south her entire life, she'd never felt protected the way she did with Malik.

"Shit," she mumbled to herself. She didn't have her keys. She usually didn't need them because she could get access with her garage door opener. Malik exited his vehicle and made his way up to where she stood on her porch.

"Everything good?"

"I'm gonna call a ride to take me to my car. I need my garage door opener." Claudia's face was full of disappointment. She wanted nothing more than to soak in her bathtub and sleep through the coming day.

"You know I can't let you call a car at this time in the morning. Ride with me, and I'll take you back."

"Are you s—"

"Claudia, get your difficult ass back in the car. You think I'm gonna let your fine ass get in another man's car, when I know you ain't got on any panties. Hell, I know because I ripped 'em off you." He entered her personal space, and she welcomed his presence. Claudia had her back against the front door as she took him in.

Malik's hand rested against her house as he leaned in to place another kiss to her lips. When he pulled away, she smiled.

"Let's go, Ms. Vaughn."

She giggled and followed him back to his truck.

* * *

MALIK STOPPED at his job to drop off the delivery truck and pick up his personal ride. Claudia hoped he wouldn't be in trouble because of her once again, due to his late middle of the night arrival. He'd only had the job for one day. Malik assured her it was fine as long as his car or the truck remained on the premises. No longer exasperated with his relaxed stride, she enjoyed the view of his gait.

He moved with the energy of a boss, though that wasn't his current work title. Claudia internally scolded herself for her quick change in perspective. Had he hypnotized her with his mystical dick? She wore a shy smirk on her face as her mind replayed their heated encounter.

Malik's car was nothing like she'd envisioned. It was an all-black, classy, luxury vehicle. Though she was positive he'd had his speakers enhanced, it wasn't full of accessories like she'd assumed it would be. She'd mischaracterized him terribly. No wonder he thought her offer was a handout. Maybe she had been out to dissolve her guilt. Claudia felt tears threaten to sting her eyes.

"You good?" he asked when he settled himself in the front seat.

"Yeah, just tired," she lied.

"I got you." Malik threw a wink her way and pulled his car out of the Postbuddies parking lot and navigated toward her home. His smartphone was safely nestled in the dock attached to his dash. The phone illuminated the space when the contact saved as Bestie popped up.

Claudia rolled her eyes when she saw it. It was barely four a.m. Malik didn't belong to her, and she knew she didn't have any business fucking him. But she expected him to have the decency not to feel the need to hide his hookups. He was a single man... wasn't he?

"It's my sister. I gotta take this," Malik threw in her direction.

46

Claudia wasn't convinced until he accepted the call on speaker, and she heard a panicked voice on the other end.

"What's up, Kita?" Malik asked. He rubbed his eyes like he could use a good night's sleep.

"It's John. He's at the house, causing a scene. If he keeps it up, he's gonna wake Daddy. And Daddy's gonna call the cops or go for his gun." Her voice trembled, and she sounded shaken.

In the background, a male voice that likely belonged to John could be heard hurling loud threats in Kita's direction.

"I'm on my way." Malik ended the call and made an abrupt turn. His jaw was clenched, and Claudia wondered what she'd gotten herself into. She didn't know shit about this man or his family.

"I don't want to be in the way," Claudia started. What was she supposed to do? She was afraid to ask him about it, but the last thing she wanted was to be a distraction.

"You won't. Just let me take care of my sister, and I'll drop you off."

Malik kept his eyes trained on the road ahead of him. His car handled each curve nicely, and it appeared to Claudia like he knew the area like the back of his hand.

The neighborhood Malik arrived at was esthetically pleasing and gated. He punched in the code, and without turning toward her, he said, "This is my folks' place."

"It's nice."

"Please be quiet," he pleaded.

"What did I do now?" Claudia crossed her arms firmly over her chest.

"You're so damn judgmental. You may as well have said you thought I was on government assistance, and I grew up without my dad."

Claudia sat wordlessly.

"I can't deal with this shit right now, Claudia. Do you have a dad?" Malik rounded several corners swiftly to make it to his sister.

"Of course."

"Why would you *assume* I didn't? Why would you assume my parents couldn't live in a place nicer than yours? They've worked a hell of a lot longer than you, Ms. Vaughn." The frustration in his voice stung, and she had no doubt she deserved it.

This time when he spoke, he'd allowed his eyes to meet hers. Claudia felt like shit because he was right. She'd decided with the way he spoke and the position he held, he'd likely come from humble beginnings. All the time she'd spent with the Butners had rubbed off on her. But it wouldn't even be fair to blame them.

Claudia spent way too long wrapped up in her own pity and sorrow, she'd lost the ability to see others clearly—especially a gem like Malik Malone. *Shit!*

He pulled up to the outside of a sizable two-story home. The home had an inviting energy and looked like the people who lived in it felt loved. It was a stark contrast to the sterile estate her folks lived in. For a moment, she envied the support she was sure Malik received from his family.

The warmth of the home contradicted the tense energy between the two adults in an argument in the driveway. A man pointed in the face of who Claudia assumed was Malik's sister with the way Malik's body seethed with anger. The woman resembled Malik, and it made Claudia do a double take between them.

Malik sat eerily quiet as he took in the scene between his sister and her man. It was as if he wanted to give her the space to work things out on her own before he intervened. Claudia could hear the volatile exchange through the half-cracked window on the passenger side of Malik's car. The man accused Markita of fooling around with one of his friends.

"Landis asked about John John. That was it. He said he hadn't heard from you in a while, and he wanted to make sure everything was good," she pleaded.

"What the fuck you doing entertaining another man's questions about my damn son? Your response should've been to tell him to ask me," he roared.

"How did you even see my messages, John?" Markita's arms were folded in front of her body as if she'd experienced a myriad of emotions.

"Don't change the subject. I been had your passwords on social media."

"But I didn't give them to you, jackass."

That was when John's hand found Markita's neck. Malik jumped out of the car, while Claudia stayed planted in her seat, praying things wouldn't escalate more than they already had. Maybe Malik's presence would be enough to motivate John to leave.

"You lost your got damn mind if you think I'm gonna let you put your filthy hands on my sister!" Malik growled. He moved with the disposition of a killer. As inappropriate as her timing was, Claudia admired how he still spoke in an even tone and used a measured cadence. His southern accent made her center throb. John should have been worried though.

"Bitch, you called your brother on me?" John was bigger than Markita, and his hand remained wrapped around her throat. She swatted at his hands like it had become difficult for her to breathe.

Malik was in his face in a split second, and his proximity caused John to release his hold on Markita. Her body doubled over, attempting to pull in air. When Malik turned his head to check on her, John snuck him with a swift punch. Claudia winced. The sound of the strike was loud and looked painful.

Malik tackled him to the ground, unbothered that John's body hit the pavement forcefully. With his knee in John's chest, Malik lifted him by the hair and commenced to punch and bitch slap him like some sort of pimp superhero. The whacks were so powerful, Claudia looked away.

"OK, Malik. Let him up," his sister begged.

Malik continued the assault, until her words seemed to penetrate.

"Just let him get the fuck out of here," she went on.

Malik nodded, satisfied he'd sent a strong enough message. Just as Malik shifted his body, John took his foot and kicked at Malik's leg, barely missing his knee. Claudia could see Malik's face turn cold. He lifted his shirt, and though she may have been a bit out of touch, she knew exactly what time it was.

She exited the car, unsure of where to go. Should she approach? Should she call out? Claudia didn't want to distract Malik while he was in a zone, but things were different now.

"Malik, no," she pleaded from the front lawn.

He didn't move his eyes. What the hell did she want? This clearly wasn't a situation open for an amicable discussion. John had choked Markita, and he would pay with his life for that shit.

"Baby," Claudia continued. The soft tone of her usually nagging voice tugged at his heart. It was the last thing he wanted while his hand rested on the cold handle of his pistol. John had his hands raised at both sides of his ears in surrender, aware that he'd gone too far this time. And Markita sobbed quietly as she watched.

"Not now, Claudia!" If she was on some 'you have too much to lose' shit, she could take it straight to hell, where Malik was willing to go for his sister. Fuck this dude.

"The baby." Claudia didn't know who the child belonged to. He shared a strong enough resemblance to be Malik's or Markita's son. She would worry about that later. What they needed to know was that he stood at the door with a blanket as Malik was about to shoot John.

All eyes flew to the door and connected with a pair of tiny innocent ones.

"John John!" Markita squealed. She rushed to his side and pressed his face into her side as Malik stood and lowered his shirt.

"Get your ass off my property. Know my nephew is the only reason I didn't spray your fucking brain into the cement." Malik's voice was low, but Claudia could appreciate every word, because she'd approached them. She didn't know what she'd do, but she wouldn't let Malik murder a man in front of a child.

She'd forgotten she was practically naked until John's eyes connected with her bare thighs. She suddenly felt exposed and tugged on the bottom of Malik's sweater as if it would magically make it longer. Malik pushed out a frustrated breath and reached out to choke John, confident the boy couldn't see.

"How does it feel to be the one getting choked? I know one thing; you best keep your damn hands off my sister and your raggedy ass eyes off my muthafuckin woman."

Claudia's heart skipped a beat. She was convinced Malik had gotten caught up in his adrenaline, but the sound of him referring to her as his woman made her insides flutter.

She walked up to him and placed her thin hand on his free but flexed bicep. Malik was in total fight mode but removed his hand from John's neck when he felt Claudia at his side. John coughed loudly as he hustled to his car. He still had a hand on his neck as he hopped in and sped off.

"Get back in the car," Malik demanded.

She wanted to protest but thought better of it. If she were clothed, she'd call a car so he could be with his sister. She didn't seem like she needed to be alone.

"I will, but maybe... maybe I can sit quietly inside while you stay with your sister until she's settled."

Malik stared at her as his mind contemplated her suggestion. His head was all over the place. Claudia had come in clutch—in a situation he was sure should have had her rocking in a corner somewhere. He half expected her to be the one to call the law. But she didn't; she was beside him, despite the danger involved in his situation. Claudia may have saved both John and his lives with her intervention.

Claudia stood quietly with a level of patience foreign to her normal 'do now, think later' pace. She wanted to support Malik however he needed; she would wait.

Malik nodded. "You're right. If you come inside, I can take my time with them without worrying if you're good out here, butt ass naked."

She smiled, and against his best efforts, he did too. He reached out and pulled her to him. "Thank you."

"You're welcome."

Six

MARKITA HAD colorful bruises on her neck, and Claudia could almost reach out and touch the pain Malik felt when he saw them. He made her promise to get herself checked out at the hospital whenever she woke up. She reluctantly agreed. Once Malik was sure Markita was OK, he took the time to introduce Claudia. He found her a pair of his shorts and passed them to her as inconspicuous as possible.

He and Claudia waited at the house, until Kita and his nephew were asleep, before they left. Claudia was touched by the gentleness Malik used with his sister and her son. He seemed more like a father to John John than an uncle.

The car ride from his parents' home to her abandoned car was uninterrupted by words. Claudia's mind raced as she tried to wrap her head around all that had gone down in her life in less than twenty-four hours.

Once Malik pulled over behind her car, she used her car keys to unlock it to retrieve her garage door opener. Her car was less than two years old and unlikely to have any issues, so she didn't feel the need to carry both car keys *and* keys to her home. Her mother had told her since she was young that a woman shouldn't jingle. With her mother's philosophy drilled in her head, Claudia decided the less keys she had, the better.

She sat back in the car and strapped herself in.

"You've wasted a lot of gas on me tonight."

A slow smile spread across Malik's handsome face. "Yeah, I have." Claudia could hear the heaviness in his voice, and she yearned to alleviate it for him.

"I..." she started.

He turned his head to look at her. "What's up?"

"Nothing," she lied.

They pulled back onto the familiar, poorly lit Georgia back roads until they reached her housing division. Claudia's eyes somehow drifted closed, and she'd fallen into an unexpected sleep.

When Claudia felt Malik put the car into park, she knew they'd arrived at her home, confident she'd be able to get in this time.

"Do you want to stay?"

"I don't think it's a good idea, Claudia Vaughn." Malik's tone was playful, but his eyes were distant.

"Let me rephrase that. Will you come in? I don't want to be alone." The sultry change in Claudia's voice was unintentional. She wanted him, but only if he wanted her too.

"I'm tired as shit. How 'bout I lay with you for a little while?"

"Please do."

They piled out of his car and entered her home through her garage. Claudia knew she'd have a hell of a day whenever she finally woke up. She'd have to deal with her car, with work, and whatever this was she started with Malik Malone. But after the night she'd just had, she wanted nothing more than to be held tightly in his strong embrace.

* * *

"CLAUDIA VAUGHN."

She cracked one eye open to see where she was. The lustrous sun was in full effect and seemed to attack her from every direction. She lifted her head from the bed to retrieve her pillow, then covered her face with it dramatically.

"Aye, girl," Malik said with laughter in his voice.

Claudia hummed her response.

"I wanted to let you know I was on the way out."

"What time is it?" she asked from beneath the pillow. Malik chuckled because her words came out muffled.

"It's officially Thursday. And it's one in the afternoon."

Claudia peeked from under the pillow, and the sight tickled Malik. "I convinced my boss to let me work later this evening, but I wanted to see what you need to take care of your car first."

"Malik, you've done plenty. I have it handled, and this time, I'll be fully dressed when I do."

"You better." His voice sounded territorial, and Claudia wasn't sure why she liked it.

She finally sat up, and attempted to smooth her unruly tresses. "Speaking of... About last night in my truck."

Claudia looked away. Was he about to tell her it shouldn't have happened? She didn't think she could handle hearing him say those words, when she desperately wanted to do it again.

"What about it?"

"Can I get your number?" Malik held his breath and tried to display confidence, though he was scared as shit.

She smiled brightly. "OK."

She gave him her number while they walked to the door. He leaned his head in her direction and took his time as he kissed her pouty lips.

"I'll call you, Claudia Vaughn," he said as he sauntered down her steps.

"You do that, Malik Malone."

Claudia's phone rang and interrupted her view of the back of Malik's toned body. He strolled to his car with the infamous gait responsible for the moisture gathered between her legs.

She tore her eyes from Malik and reentered her home to where her cell was plugged into the charger. When she picked it up, she saw she had several missed calls and texts from Nick, her work mentor. She'd texted him early this morning and said she wouldn't be on any virtual meetings today because she had some personal things come up.

Apparently, Nick was worried because he'd called an obscene amount of times.

"Hey." She sighed into the phone. Drama filled or not, she had one of the best nights of her life with Malik.

To top things off, she was just as satisfied with them sleeping atop the covers, fully clothed, because he held her in his powerful arms. Malik maintained his tight grip on her as they slept. The one time she got up to use the bathroom, she had to wiggle to get out of his grasp. The moment she'd returned, he pulled her into him like he missed her.

"I've been worried sick!" Nick exclaimed.

She pulled the phone from her face, surprised at the way he'd spoken to her like she was a child.

"I appreciate your concern," she said as gently as she could manage. "But I'm not sure why you were worried. I sent you a message letting you know I wouldn't be on today."

Nick blew out a frustrated breath, and before Claudia could address it, she got a text from an unknown number.

"Hold on a second." She put the call on speaker to give her better access to her screen.

555-6723: *plug me in*

Claudia had a feeling it was Malik, but he'd just left. She prayed he didn't have a habit of texting and driving.

Claudia: *Who is this?*

555-6723: *dis the daddy*

Claudia giggled to herself as her mind recalled how Malik had proclaimed he was the daddy now while he was inside of her. Her eyes closed briefly, and she felt welcomed flutters in her stomach.

Claudia: *Huh?*

555-6723: *I ripped those pretty panties last night*

Before Claudia could stop herself, she responded with a water droplet emoji.

Nick cleared his throat. She had forgotten he was on the line.

"My apologies. Like I said before, I have some personal things that need my attention, but I'll be available tomorrow." Her patience was thin. She'd always had easy conversations with Nick and considered him an ally who understood her amidst colleagues who seemed to speak an entirely different language.

"I was worried because this isn't like you to suddenly need time away without explanation."

Claudia found herself a bit offended by his statement. Had she become a workaholic of sorts? Was she so laser-focused on the job that he was surprised she could have a personal issue she wasn't interested in sharing?

"I understand. Again, thank you for your concern. I've had a long night, and I'd love to continue our conversation tomorrow." Claudia was strictly professional. It was a tone she didn't historically take with Nick, but he'd never behaved entitled to access the personal details of her life either.

"OK, I'll see you tomorrow, Claudia."

Claudia said goodbye and disconnected the call. When she opened up her texts, she had another message from Malik.

555-6723: *you liked it? I could do it again*

Before she could respond, Claudia programmed a pseudonym for Malik into her contacts. She hadn't felt giddy about a man since college.

Claudia: *maybe you should*

Hood Body Briefs: *damn girl! Let me text you when my nephew ain't around. You a bad influence.*

Claudia: you *like it*

Hood Body Briefs: *maybe I do. I need to go, but can I take you out this weekend*

Claudia: *yes*

Claudia was over the moon with excitement. A date with Malik Malone. What had she gotten herself into?

Seven

IT WAS a sunny Saturday afternoon when Claudia pulled her car into the location Malik sent her. Her neck craned to appreciate the impossibly tall maple trees. The sounds of birds and other wildlife sang angelic praises as she exited her vehicle. She'd once again misjudged Malik when he suggested their first date be a hike.

Dumbfounded, she agreed to his nontraditional meetup, though she was slightly disappointed she didn't have on a fitted 'fuck me' dress. Small sticks cracked beneath her sneakers as she passed a wilderness sign that detailed the woodland creatures she might see on the trail. Though she and Red were tight as ever, she had no desire to see other snakes in their natural habitat.

Claudia had made it a few more yards before Malik's masculine frame came into her field of view. *My, my, my, he is fine.* A lazy grin played across his face—she would have sworn he was genuinely happy to see her. As he neared, he scratched the area between his eyebrow and hairline.

"I told you I was taking you on a hike," he said as he surveyed her outfit.

"I know. What's wrong with this?" Malik's laughter was slow and thunderous. Claudia popped her hip to one side and rolled her eyes upward. "It's not like I came in heels. What's wrong with it?" she whined.

He ambled in her direction with a small chuckle.

"Yeah, but you're not wearing long sleeves. And where are your boots?" Malik spun her around to get a view of her backside. "Damn if you don't look good enough to eat though."

Claudia wore a dark colored pair of fresh sneakers. She figured it was what she'd wear on a walk, and since there was a possibility there would be mud on the trail, she decided against the white shoes she thought matched her outfit better. She thought she was plenty prepared.

Malik had never dealt with a woman like Claudia Vaughn before. While he enjoyed her attire, it was obvious she had no idea what to wear on a hike. Her outfit made sense for those sexy twerkouts, but for the woods, she looked out of place as hell. He admired her body one last time before he decided to break the news to her.

"Baby," he started. Claudia's smile widened at the endearment—and the slow southern way he said baby—but faltered as he continued. "While I think one short and one long leg is uniquely sexy for yoga pants, it's not the best 'fit for the woods. There will be mosquitoes and ticks in these woods, and some of the branches have thorns."

She crossed her arms over her chest as she took in Malik's attire. She'd been terribly distracted by his face and the way his eyes were on her. Now it was clear what he meant since he wore clothes that covered his arms and legs, and he had hiking boots on his feet.

"I have a hoodie in my car." Claudia ran back to her car and retrieved a sweater to put his criticism to rest.

Malik's teasing laughter annoyed her and oddly turned her on.

"What now?" she asked with the super crop top resting on her shoulders. It was a black cut-off hoodie that stopped above the breast line of her neon-colored tank. There was a space between the bottom of the hoodie and the shirt she wore under it.

"Did you cut this sweater?"

"No. I bought it like this. It covers my arms."

Malik pulled her close. He ran his finger across her chest to highlight her exposed skin, then repeated the motion at her waist, where neither her tank top nor the hoodie concealed.

"What about all of this?" He peered down at her, aware of the increase in the cadence of her breath. "Did you put on insect repellant?"

She huffed in frustration. Claudia was accustomed to doing most things well; it was rare for her to be unprepared. She hadn't considered half the things Malik mentioned. In her mind, a hike was a glorified walk.

"Was I supposed to?"

Malik removed his camo decorated backpack and pulled out a small bottle.

"Cover your eyes," he commanded.

Claudia willed her body not to respond to the texture of Malik's voice. She couldn't recall a time where she'd been led or directed by an attractive man, but she did as she was told. The cool spray of the mist settled over her uncovered areas, which were not only on her chest and midsection. Malik sprayed her wrists, ankles, and across the back of her neck.

She silently thanked God she had the good sense to tie up her hair in a headwrap with a knot at the top toward the heavens. She'd done it because she knew it was cute, but mostly because she didn't want anything to fall into her natural hair.

He returned the spray to his bag and pulled out a pair of pliers. Claudia wanted to ask what they were for, but decided she'd been schooled enough for a lifetime. She adjusted her designer sunglasses. Between her car keys that fit in a hidden pocket along her hip, and her water bottle, she hadn't brought anything else.

He nodded to one of the paths, and they made their way into the Georgia woods. After less than five minutes, Claudia was in love with her surroundings. The enormous trees with their colorful leaves and the sounds enveloped her in a much-needed hug. She'd spent too much time indoors now that she worked from home.

Malik had her walk ahead of him where the trail narrowed to fit only one hiker at a time. A twig with thorns snagged the sleeve of her hoodie. Her breath caught as Malik reached out and clipped the branch with his pliers. Claudia had attempted to strong arm the branch and yank away but only got more tangled. Even with her hoodie, the thorn bit into her skin.

He surveyed her arm, and once he was satisfied she hadn't been hurt, they continued. They didn't speak much, and Claudia was content with the silence. She'd occupied herself with the sights of the outdoors. How long would she have gone without an experience like this, had she not met him? Was she really living her life fully?

The sound of water made her face light up. Malik elbowed her playfully as he grasped her hand.

"These rocks are slick. And since you wore sneakers, you'll need to be extra careful."

She wanted to roll her eyes, but after her run-in with the branch, she thought it best to take his word for it. A beautiful waterfall washed over a section of the woods. They'd climbed a small area of rock to get a closer look. Claudia couldn't help herself, she released his grip and wandered alongside the waterfall.

She put her hands in the downpour, as if she couldn't be convinced it was real until she touched it.

"Take my picture." She walked back to Malik and shoved her smartphone in his hands.

She stood with a cheesy smile that elicited another belly laugh in Malik.

"You remind me of my sister."

"Is that a good thing?"

Malik returned her phone and brushed debris off her shoulder.

"She's my favorite person in the world. It's a damn good thing."

Claudia's mood shifted as she thought of her dynamic with her own twin. "I'm a twin too."

"No, shit?"

"Yup," she responded with little enthusiasm. Claudia always felt immense shame when others learned she was a twin, because they had a strained relationship. "I have a fraternal sister, like you, but we're not close at all."

"Are you the mean one?"

She regarded him to determine if there was any hidden accusation behind his words, but he seemed to be sincere in his inquiry.

"I can be mean, but she hates me like an evil twin, if that's what you're really asking.

"I can't imagine. I don't remember a time when me and Kita weren't close."

"I could tell by the way you took care of her the other night. And by the way you treat your nephew. For a moment, I thought he was your son."

"Here you go with the stereo—"

"Not because I thought you had to be somebody's baby daddy. I thought you were his dad because his little face is like a carbon copy of yours. He also looked at you like you hung the stars."

Malik's face softened as they discussed his family.

"I feel like he is my son. I love that kid more than I love myself."

Claudia's eyes drifted above Malik's head and connected with a crimson-colored bird. She'd never seen a cardinal in person. She took an unexpected step forward and lost her footing. Before her butt hit the rock, Malik was there to catch her. Their eyes connected, and the intimate nature of their closeness made her feel exposed.

She regained her balance and stood. Claudia created a comfortable distance between them which caused Malik to wonder what the hell Butner had done in their marriage to make her feel the need to keep her guard up. She'd been uninhibited in the back of his work truck, but a harmless embrace seemed to be off limits.

"Tell me about your sister. What's her name?"

Claudia crouched down and mindlessly ran a twig against a rock. Malik rather enjoyed the childlike side of her. He bent his wide frame and took a seat beside the woman who had his full attention.

"Victoria Vaughn. Sounds like a famous actress, doesn't it?"

Malik nodded. He willed himself to focus on her words as he studied the texture of her hair and the way the irises of her eyes appeared two shades lighter under the sun. She'd pushed her sunglasses to rest atop her thick tresses.

"She's always been a star. She'd perform for anyone's attention. Vicky did all the church plays and local theater productions since she was four. It was like she was born to do it."

Malik reached over and pulled a leaf from her hair as she spoke. He berated himself for being so tender with her because it generally wasn't his style. "Where did you fit into all of this?"

Claudia sighed. "I love my sister. I've been her biggest fan since the beginning. I've gone to almost every live show she's done. The sad part is, as we got older, I hid and pretended I wasn't there to avoid unnecessary drama. She'd probably accuse me of trying to sabotage her." Claudia rolled her eyes as she told the story.

"Once the pandemic hit, she started doing voiceover work."

"No shit?"

"Yup."

"And what was Claudia Vaughn like?"

The conversation felt more intimate than the embrace Malik held her in when she lost her footing. She'd enjoyed getting to know him in a short amount of time, but her history and track record with men said she needed to guard her heart.

"I'm the smart one. While Vicky memorized scenes from popular movies, I was in the corner reading intense nonfiction books about investing for children or how to score high on college placement exams."

Malik's laughter seemed to echo off the rock surrounding them. "That sounds exactly like how I'd picture you. But when you say it like that, it actually sounds kind of cute."

Claudia had taken a seat next to Malik once she tired of her mindless activity with the stick. She craned her neck to face him, and without a second thought, he leaned in and placed a kiss on her lips.

She pulled back, and a light giggle escaped her lips.

"What's so funny, Ms. Vaughn?" Malik wore a flirtatious grin as he awaited her response.

"It's just that I've never gotten this type of response for being the way I am with my family. They're all creative and fluid, so my desire to create and grow money makes no sense to them. Vicky saw my things laid out at our parents' house one day. I can't remember why I was working there, but I was. She ran across a ten thousand dollar check I wrote to a women's shelter.

"Vicky accused me of trying to buy my way out of guilt for being greedy. She said I was a corporate snob, and just because I threw money at those people, it didn't mean I cared.

"I wish they could understand that making money and investing in other people's dreams *is* my version of creativity."

He adjusted himself and stood. Once he was up, he held his hand out to assist her. Claudia grabbed Malik's hand and allowed him to pull her to her feet.

"Thank you for being open with me about your people. I think it's dope that you're not selfish with the money you make."

Her smile was bright and mischievous.

"What's that look for?"

"Now will you let me introduce you to some of the affluent investors I know?"

Malik put his hand in his pocket in search of a toothpick but had no luck. He was out and wondered if he had some in his car. "I'll think about it."

Claudia jumped up and down, squealing as she did. It was a pleasant surprise for Malik to see a different side of her. A week ago, he'd wanted to choke the shit out of her. Things had shifted—he was quite smitten with Claudia Vaughn.

They turned to head back toward the cars since they'd already been gone for an hour. He shared a granola bar with her when he heard her stomach rumble. She admitted she'd skipped breakfast and only had a protein shake.

They hiked a good amount of the walk back in silence. A snicker from Claudia regained Malik's attention.

"What's so funny, girl?" he asked as he playfully tugged at the band of her pants.

"I never told you what happened to my car."

"What happened?"

"I can't remember the last time I had an oil change. I don't think I've gotten one since I bought the car a year and a half ago."

Malik stopped. His facial expression was serious. "What?"

She ran her hand across the stubble on his jaw. "I know."

He momentarily forgot why he was upset with the contact of her hand against his face. He secretly loved the sensation and wished she hadn't stopped. He regained his composure and added, "You forgot to change your oil? What about the light on your dashboard?"

Claudia took in Malik's tendency to scratch his head between his brow and hairline anytime he wanted to have an emotional outburst.

She figured he would give himself a bruise there by the end of their time together with the way she pushed him to the limit. The southern elements of Malik's protective personality were unfamiliar within the context of the new association they'd formed.

Her maternal grandparents were from the west, so although she'd lived her entire life in Georgia, her mother hadn't. People in Claudia's family and world were spirited. They had places to go and opportunities to take. Malik was her first encounter with a man who could be both driven and unhurried in his everyday interactions with others.

He'd kept his eyes on her as her mind wandered and compared the many differences in the way they both showed up in the world. His patience was on full display. She got the impression her unresponsiveness to her vehicle and her safety had him frustrated with her. It was cute.

"The check oil light had been on for so long—I'd ignored it all together. If I'm honest, I don't think I even knew what the light was."

He leaned his head toward the heavens in irritation. It was as if Claudia's words took him to a place he didn't like to be. He couldn't protect her if she was careless with something as basic as routine car maintenance—not that it was his job.

"Let's finish this walk before I spank your ass." His jaw clenched, but Claudia was... aroused. She couldn't tell if he'd meant it to sound sexual in nature, but that was certainly how her body had taken it.

Who the hell is this man?

* * *

THEY FINISHED their hike in just under two hours. Claudia's muscles ached in a most welcomed way, because she loved to walk and workout. She considered adding "hike" to her list of preferred fitness. She leaned against her car as she took in his frame.

Malik had the face and the body of a god. His likeness should be replicated and placed in a museum for humans to admire for years to come. How the hell had she gone from despising this man to lusting after him in the worst way? Malik's clothes were powerless to hide the ripped outlines of his arms and legs. He hadn't even broken a sweat.

"I want to see you again, Claudia," he said. Malik's gaze fixated on her lips as he made his declaration.

She unconsciously tucked hers between her teeth. "OK."

The ring of her cell phone sounded simultaneously with the massive grin on Malik's face. Claudia stood from her restful position near her car. "This is work. Give me a second."

"Handle your business, Ms. Vaughn." Malik took the opportunity to admire her ass in her one short leg and one full-length leg, pair of yoga pants. They were like a mashup of shorts and pants. *Did she get those custom made? Shit!* He decided to retrieve his phone to distract himself from his salacious thoughts and to see if he had any missed calls or emails that required his attention. Claudia's light giggles interrupted his scroll. *What the hell?*

"It's not a problem. I can send it when I get back to my car. Yes, it has oil," she said into the phone.

It didn't sound like work to Malik. Her response to whoever the hell was on her phone had her almost as relaxed as he'd made her. What the hell was he supposed to do in this situation? She didn't belong to him, although he was convinced her body did. Malik figured since she was divorced and clearly still affected by it, that she was single.

Shit! The last thing Malik needed was to get twisted up in some rich people drama. He hadn't even taken the time to search her name on the internet. Maybe she'd gotten a divorce because she was the one who cheated on a Butner. Claudia was a beautiful and surprisingly freaky woman.

She returned to face him in less than two minutes. She gave him a quick smile than tapped away on her phone. After another moment or so, he snatched it.

"Hey," she said as she unsuccessfully tried to get it back.

"I'm not OK sharing your attention with anybody else." His tone was even. She realized this was a boundary of his and one she didn't mind accepting, but the sound of his words made her body tremble with desire.

"Did you want to make plans now? Or do you just want to call me later?" Claudia spoke through her body's response to him. She hadn't wanted to sound eager, but she wouldn't let her pride keep her from an opportunity to see him again. The email to Nick could wait.

"I don't know."

Her smile faltered at the tortured sound of his voice. "OK."

He blew out a breath. Why did he suddenly feel as though he was in high school, jealous because his girlfriend let another boy carry her books. "What was that about just now?" His hand raked across the top of his low-cut hair. It was another one of those peculiar things he did to regulate himself.

"Are you talking about Nick?"

Malik did the slow nod that made Claudia want to scream. *Because apparently Miss Kitty suddenly likes a country boy.*

"He's a colleague who is my mentor in the company, but more like a friend of the family."

"Yeah, well I couldn't hear what he said, but the way you sounded made me think he was trying to put you in a good mood. It's the same shit I'm over here doing."

Claudia smiled at his words—about him trying to put her in a good mood. She'd willingly had sex with him while she was beyond pissed off. He didn't have to worry about whether she was in a good mood or not, but she found it sweet he felt the need.

"I'm not attracted to Nick. He's an almost sixty-year-old white man. Not my type."

"Right." He'd spoken his piece and didn't have anything else to say about the matter.

"Anyway. What did you say about seeing me later?"

Malik liked that she hadn't chosen to beat around the bush. He'd been laser-focused on his goals in life, but now that he'd met her, he wanted a little balance.

"I don't feel like dealing with a lot of people. Let me come over tonight. I'll bring some food, and we can just chill at your place, if that's cool with you."

Claudia didn't try to hide her excitement. She stepped forward and enclosed her arms around his neck. He closed his eyes when he felt her body pressed against his. Claudia took the initiative to kiss him on her own accord.

"I'm gonna go shower and do a little work until our dinner date."

He kissed her again. "I'm surprised your ass doesn't require a five star, hundred-dollar plate type of dinner date," he said as he licked the taste of her on his lips.

She slipped from his embrace, then added, "We can do that next weekend."

She winked and turned to get into her car.

"Drive safely, Claudia."

"Will do."

Eight

MALIK COULDN'T REMEMBER the last time he was off on a Saturday night. Apparently, neither could his family.

"Is it the girl with the legs?" his sister asked as she buzzed around him. Despite the traumatic chain of events, she'd remembered the attractive, chocolate girl who'd worn her brother's hooded sweatshirt.

"Kita, I'm trying to get dressed."

"A hoodie is barely dressed. You still cute though."

He turned to face her. "Yes, I'm gonna pick up some food and hang out with Claudia tonight."

"You must really like her, to be buying her food."

Malik returned his brush to the bathroom drawer and gave himself one last look. "I think I do. But I've only known her for like a week."

"She came here with no draws on. I think you know her fairly well."

"Get out, man," Malik said, although he was unable to conceal his laughter. "I'll be back later. Tell everybody I said I love 'em."

Malik's parents had taken John John out for the evening to give Markita a break. She was on her way to lie down when she'd gotten sidetracked with Malik's plans.

"OK, big head. You got protection?"

"That's it!" Malik picked her up and walked her down the hallway to her room.

"Don't you dare."

Malik easily lifted Kita above his head then dropped her onto the bed.

"I can't stand you!" She yelled with a voice full of laughter.

"I farted in there too!" he yelled as he reached the front door.

"Malik Malone! I'm tellin' Mama."

He didn't give her an opportunity to say anything else, because he closed the door. The evening temperature felt like the perfect running weather. Malik didn't usually have the time to run at night, and as he got in his car, he wondered if Claudia was the type of woman who might accompany him for an impromptu workout.

Malik made the drive to one of his favorite Jamaican restaurants. Traffic was light like it always was in the evening of their small town. The closer he drove to Atlanta, the more chaotic it would get. But the restaurant he'd chosen for pickup was on the outer limits of the busy city.

Although Malik had been committed to avoiding people for the day, there was no way around it if he didn't want some random person handling his food in their car. He knew about that life because it was what he did for a living. So, he found himself in a semi-packed Ma and Pops styled eatery.

The place was small, which meant the capacity was low. Malik decided to have a drink at the bar while he waited for their orders. He ordered a jerk chicken with rice and peas and cabbage for himself. For Claudia, he ordered the brown stew chicken with the same sides, except he opted for greens in place of the cabbage. He had a feeling she wouldn't enjoy spicy food.

He'd taken in his surroundings and looked beyond the overly made-up women. None of those superficial qualities, like skin-deep aesthetics, interested him anymore. Malik wanted something solid in his professional life, and once he had it, he wanted to share it with someone real.

"Hey, buddy. You mind letting my wife have this seat."

Malik smoothed the lines that formed above his brow as the pretentious voice boomed in his ear. Of course, he didn't mind yielding his seat for a lady, especially a pregnant one. It was the sound of her man's abrasive tone that had him tense.

He stood and helped the woman onto the stool. She'd wobbled like her short legs and displaced body weight wouldn't allow her to sit comfortably.

"Thank you," the woman said.

"Not a problem. You good?" Malik was afraid to release her. He didn't want any problems after the last domestic dispute he'd been involved in with his sister's baby daddy. But here he was, alongside another vulnerable woman and a man who couldn't care less.

"She's fine. She doesn't need help sitting down. I don't know why everyone acts like she has a disability. She's pregnant, not crippled."

The hell did this asshole just say?

The woman shook her head as if to warn Malik not to engage. She was beautiful, but the vacant look in her eyes was similar to the one he'd seen in his sister's. Malik's head throbbed. He knew he'd have to leave it up to her whether she allowed her man to continue his toxic behavior.

He'd gotten a few steps toward a quiet table by the window, when the waiter called out, "Tommy Butner."

Malik's head jerked up so fast he thought he had whiplash. He watched as the tall all-American-built asshole yanked at his wife's frail frame. He practically dragged her with him as they were seated. Malik was more than familiar with the high ratings and national reviews the restaurant received, but still hadn't imagined he'd run into the golden boy Tommy Butner.

No wonder Claudia was the way she was. Malik didn't fool himself to think Butner was the reason for all her flaws, but the venom toward men and her fear around intimacy with him made a hell of a lot more sense. If he had to guess, Claudia's slick tongue was innately hers. Malik chuckled to himself at the thought of Claudia's foul mouth, despite his headache from the overexposure to peopling.

He'd fucked her until she agreed to speak nicely to him. God only knew if she could keep her word.

"Malone," a girl dressed in all black called out.

He threw her a nod and swaggered in her direction. Malik handed her a tip once he'd made it back to the bar. He quickly peered into the bag to ensure their food was correct. "Thank you."

"Not a problem. You have yourself a nice evening." The girl who was probably twenty years old gave Malik the "fuck me" eyes, but there was only one person he wanted to fuck, and he was on his way to her place right fucking now.

* * *

THE DRIVE to Claudia's home from the restaurant took Malik around thirty minutes. He'd propped their food in his passenger side after he'd made makeshift holes in the sides of their to-go containers to vent their food. He wanted to ensure the contents weren't soggy the first time she had it.

Malik was deep in thought as he carried the bag toward her front door. In less than a week's time, he went from hating her to wanting nothing more than to be inside of her. His knocks at her front door were met with what sounded like a hushed conversation. *The hell?*

He'd texted her that he was on the way. Was one of her family members inside? The thought put a smile on his face. He'd pay money to see Claudia bent out of shape over someone other than him. As long as it was harmless in nature, he'd get a kick out of it.

She opened the door, and he took his time as he scanned her from head to toe. Claudia was dressed in a simple, gray lounge dress. It was the perfect outfit for an at-home date. But the way she wore it would result in the two of them reenacting scenes from that night in his truck.

The short length of the ribbed knitted dress hit just above her succulent thighs. Claudia had the type of legs that made Malik want to scream. She'd taken the time to lather herself in a lemon, coconut, and shea body butter. He knew because he smelled her the moment she opened the door. The dress was fitted at the top and swung loosely around her hips.

Her natural hair was full and untamed. Claudia's wild mane was a stark contrast to the personality he recalled from the first time he'd graced her steps. Malik stood there frozen as he continued to take her in.

Her feet were uncovered, and he winced when he saw how beautiful they were. Malik didn't have high standards when it came to a woman's feet. If they were clean and didn't stink, he didn't discriminate. He figured they'd carried her around all damn day, they deserved the right to look beat up. But Claudia's toes looked like maybe he wouldn't mind putting them in his mouth. *What the fuck am I thinking?*

She waited patiently for him to speak.

As he fumbled with the bag, he said, "I brought dinner."

"It smells divine. Come on in."

"OK."

She turned away from him, and it took all the restraint he had not to lift her dress and fuck her right there in her foyer. Though he felt in a daze at the sight of her backside, he faintly recalled she had company or was on a call.

"Who do we have here?"

Malik immediately shifted his gaze to the man seated at the substantial dining room table. Though it had been early in the morning the last time Malik was there, he remembered it—he thought it would be a good place to take Claudia when he needed to remind her who was boss.

The older man stood and held out his hand. He looked much younger than Malik expected when Claudia told him the man was in his sixties. He had a gray beard and a neatly trimmed salt and pepper colored haircut. It was obvious buddy groomed himself well and made regular visits to the gym and the barber.

He wore relaxed white jeans and a navy-blue blazer like he was here on a date. And why the hell was he at Claudia's? He'd already interrupted their hike earlier. Malik left Nick's long muscular arm suspended in the air and returned it with a slow nod. He could see the disgust in her mentor's eyes as Malik slowly followed behind Claudia.

Malik didn't work for him, and he damn sure didn't owe him any pleasantries. It was clear ole boy wanted to fuck her, and he'd banked on the fact she didn't have a clue. With Malik in the picture, Nick knew it was a wrap.

When Claudia turned to face him, he met her with a mouth full of the diamonds she'd grown to love. He couldn't keep his smile from her if he tried.

She blushed as she grabbed the food and placed it on the kitchen counter. "Baby, I want you to meet my mentor, Nick."

"I wanna meet you," Malik said as he pulled her plush body against his.

Claudia's ears orgasmed at the slow and steady way Malik spoke to her. "He can hear us." Though they had entered the kitchen, the open concept allowed for easy movement between the spaces. If Nick took just a few steps, he'd see Malik with two handfuls of her ass.

"I don't give a fuck about that. I told you I don't want to share your attention." He kissed the side of her neck between his words.

"We're just about finished. Come sit with me."

"Fine."

Claudia pulled herself from Malik's embrace and reentered the dining area where Nick stood with a red, yellow, and black snake wrapped around his arm.

"What the fuck?" Malik asked, frozen at the entryway to the kitchen.

"It's Red."

"You know this muthafucka? Or are you pointing out one of its colors?"

Nick and Claudia laughed. Malik wanted to flatten his ass, but his feet would not move. Obviously, Claudia was familiar with the snake, but it didn't make the situation any less frightening.

"Oh, he hasn't met your baby," Nick said with a tinge of sarcasm in his voice.

Nick took a step toward Malik but stopped when his fierce words settled across the room.

"I will shoot you and that snake if you walk over here trying to be funny." Malik hadn't moved, but the evenness in which he spoke made it clear to everyone, including Red, he wasn't to be fucked with.

"Baby," Claudia started. She unwrapped the snake from Nick's arm and returned it to a wooden tank that featured a single glass wall. He'd unknowingly walked past the tank, with a red heat lamp and all the trimmings, more than once. She padded back near Malik, and with her hand rested lightly against his toned pecs, whispered her apology. "I'm sorry I didn't tell you. I own a snake. Is that a deal breaker?"

Malik wanted to be pissed, and he especially wanted to beat the brakes off the jackass who'd tried to scare him. Instead, he threw Claudia one of his panty dropping smiles. "It's gonna take more than this overly zealous old man and a garden snake to get me to leave."

"Hey, what's your problem?" Nick stood with his arms perched high on his hips like the law.

Before Malik could respond, Claudia chimed in. "I think it's time for you to go."

For some odd reason, Nick misunderstood and had a goofy grin plastered across his well moisturized face. *Muthafucka look like he spends more time in the mirror than Claudia!*

Malik bent down and placed a kiss on Claudia's cheek and left for the kitchen. Homeboy was threatened enough. He didn't need an audience when he got dismissed, because Claudia would definitely dismiss him.

"I'll be in there in a second," she called toward the kitchen.

"I mean you, Nick. What you just pulled was unnecessary. And come to think of it, I told you I had dinner plans already."

"It was a joke, Claudy."

Claudy? Malik shook his head from where he stood in the kitchen as he heard her "mentor" grovel.

"Really? who would have thought somebody that..."

"Somebody that what?" Claudia pressed.

Malik didn't have to see Claudia's face to know she was annoyed. He thought the shit was rather sexy. Finally, someone other than him would feel her wrath.

"You know what I mean. The guy's huge. Who would have guessed he'd be afraid of a little snake." Nick's voice was desperate. If he thought he'd made Malik look weak, he'd failed and only succeeded at making himself look insensitive to the woman he'd tried to impress.

"I didn't think I'd need to educate you on the implications of how problematic it is for you to comment on the size of a black man."

Nick attempted to jump in, but Claudia continued. "We can talk about this another time. Right now, I want to enjoy my date."

There was a stretch of silence between them that led Malik to poke his head in the next room to ensure nothing would pop off.

Nick gave Claudia one last pleading look before he headed to the door. After she locked up, she turned to find Malik leaned against the kitchen door frame like a bronzed god. She briefly wondered what the hell had gotten into Nick, but her rumination was interrupted by Mr. Hood Body Briefs himself.

Malik wore another one of his hooded sweatshirts that seemed to have been tailored to fit him. Along with the black hoodie, he wore a pair of gray sweatpants that should've been against the law. Claudia shamelessly gawked at him in all his glory.

"You like what you see, Ms. Vaughn?" Malik asked. The words fell out of his beautiful mouth like the two of them had a lifetime to casually chat.

Claudia was impatient with his pace but nodded her head in response to his question. She ambled in his direction with the pad of her feet against the hardwood as the only sound between them.

"Buddy definitely wants to fuck you," Malik said once Claudia stood in front of him. He hadn't touched her yet because part of him was still furious with Nick.

"He doesn't—"

"Yeah, he do, baby. But it's all good. You made your choice loud and clear when you put his ass out." Malik's lazy grin made Claudia's palms perspire.

"He was trippin'. I also didn't want you to meet Red like that."

Panic covered Malik's face.

"She won't get out, she doesn't bite, and she's nonvenomous," Claudia said, using three fingers to emphasize each of her points.

Malik scratched the area above his brow.

"You wanna come see?" Claudia asked cautiously, but with a small smile. In the short time she'd known Malik, his nonverbal language already spoke volumes. She could read him with little effort. He absolutely did not want to see, but he would appease her.

He slowly allowed Claudia to pull him in the direction of Red's tank, but the snake was nowhere to be found.

"What the hell?"

"She's behind the cork bark." She laughed when she saw the wrinkles of confusion dented in his forehead. "It looks like a log."

"If you want, you can peek over the top, or I can take her out."

Malik steadied his breath. *What the entire hell have I gotten myself into?* He wordlessly leaned up on his toes, and sure enough, there she was. She slithered out of the corner onto a stick Claudia propped up for her.

"Shit! How many snakes do you have?"

"Just the one. And before you ask, I'm not the snake version of a crazy cat lady. I went to the pet store that day to get a puppy."

Malik chuckled nervously as he stepped back from the tank. "I think I've seen enough."

"OK. Can we eat now? I'm starving."

They took turns washing their hands in her half bath. As Malik laid out the food, she promised to give him a full tour of the house once they were done. He'd only seen some of it the other night. Claudia raved about the brown stew and admitted he'd guessed accurately—she didn't enjoy spicy food.

"I saw your boy tonight."

Claudia stared at him with a dumbfounded look on her face.

"Butner boy."

She froze. *Why the hell is he talking to me about Tommy?* "Oh." Because what else was she supposed to say?

"How long ago did y'all break up?"

Claudia had lost her appetite. There was no way she would talk about Tommy without bursting into tears or turning into a raging lunatic.

"We split up two years ago, but the divorce was finalized about six months ago."

"He said that pregnant woman was his wife. The timeline ain't addin' up," Malik said in the unhurried way he always spoke.

Only Claudia didn't relish his pace as they spoke of her ex and his new wife. "Can you please stop talking?" Claudia dropped her fork and felt her stomach churn. She needed a pause button before she morphed into the bitch she'd been when he pulled up to her house with his music blaring.

"Why?"

Claudia lifted from her seat and created distance between them.

"He's obviously moved on, but you haven't?" Malik asked. His tone was accusatory, and Claudia was sensitive enough to hear it.

"I said drop it!" Claudia bit the inside of her lip. What the hell was this? She didn't want to be torn up over Tommy. The bastard cheated on her and married his mistress. And apparently, everyone knew she was with child… again.

Malik shifted his body in the chair to face her. If she wanted a Butner type of man, he wasn't the one. And he didn't give a damn how hurt she was; she would talk to him like she had some sense.

"I'mma need you to lower your voice and watch your tone when you speak to me."

Claudia's eyes were on him, and they were filled with challenge. "You're not my daddy."

He stood and took his time as he approached her. Claudia's head was all over the place. She was pissed about Tommy and ashamed at her response to Malik's questions, but now with his close proximity, she could smell her own pheromones. She averted her gaze.

He reached out and gently lifted her chin. "You like starting arguments before we fuck?"

She rolled her eyes at him. "I'm not fucking you. You can get out!" She bluffed. She didn't want him to leave, but he'd pissed her off, and Claudia never backed down.

"I should choke the shit out of your pretty ass. I know that's what you want. You're over here saying I'm not your daddy, when I know good and got damn well you remember what I said." Malik wrapped his hand gently around her neck.

Claudia moaned in response. "Said about what?"

"When I was fucking you in my truck, I told you I was the daddy now," he growled.

She swatted his hand away and looked up into his mocha-colored eyes. "Fuck you. You can leave!" She turned her back to storm off but hadn't gotten more than a few inches before Malik pulled her back to him. He put his hand between her legs and easily pushed her lace panties aside.

"Shit," he growled again. "You're so fucking wet. Your body don't want me to go."

Claudia's legs quivered under his touch. He maintained his hold on her arm as he stroked the sensitive area between her thighs. She moaned audibly, already on the brink of an orgasm.

"Tell me to leave again, Claudia," he whispered.

Her eyes rolled to the back of her head as he used his thumb to play with her sweet spot.

"You want me to go?"

She shook her head.

"You said you were gonna watch how you spoke to me. Remember that?"

She did remember, but she couldn't think straight. She was pissed and ashamed and too damn aroused. What the hell had Malik Malone done to her resolve?

His fingers stopped, and he removed them suddenly. Claudia's eyes flew open just in time to see him bring his fingers to his mouth to taste her essence. He pulled his wallet from his back pocket and removed a condom, fully aware her eyes were on him.

"What's that supposed to be? I told you to get out." Her tone betrayed her, as it was laced with desire. She knew it, and he could smell it—in the air and on his fingers.

"Fuck that. Your words is saying one thing, but your body is saying another."

"My words are saying, you're not fucking me. You're being an asshole."

"How am I being an asshole?" Malik removed his hoodie and tossed it on a nearby chair.

Claudia's eyes danced with delight. She did want him, but he should have shut his mouth when she asked him to.

"Because I asked about that clown Tommy?"

She turned her back to him again and stormed out of the kitchen. Her chest heaved with unsteadied, angry breaths. When he didn't follow her, she peeked behind her to see where he was. He stood naked except for those Hood Body Briefs that made Claudia's mouth water. He rubbed his hand across the top of his hair and patiently awaited her next move.

She lifted her lounge dress over her head and exposed a matching set of lingerie. Malik's eyes almost popped out of his head at the sight of her hot pink thong with diamond hearts on each of her hips. There was another heart at the center of her cleavage where her bra converged.

"I don't want to talk about him."

"You still hung up on Butner?"

She looked away. This was too much. They were practically naked, covered only by their underwear, and he wanted to talk about fucking Tommy.

"Your slick mouth, I can tolerate. I have a few ideas on how I can fix that. But I already said I'm not going to share your attention, and I don't like repeating myself." Malik meant what he'd said. If she was bent out of shape over a fuck boy who had another wife and baby on the way, Malik needed to know the drama she was on before he dove back inside of her. He'd fuck around and get addicted.

She covered her chest with her arms as she continued to verbally process where her head was at. "It's embarrassing," she said, barely above a whisper. She paced the floor then turned back into his direction. "And I don't fucking want to talk about it!" She yelled.

That was it. Malik had enough. He strolled in her direction and pulled her back into the kitchen. He reached out and ripped her flimsy panties. Claudia's hummed response was confirmation for him to keep it up.

He lifted her and sat her bare cheeks on the kitchen counter, then lowered to his knees. "I get it now. You're not hung up over him, you just don't want to talk. I'll let it go for now. What I'm not gonna let slide is you yelling at me."

"OK."

"OK? Hell nah. I need you to tell me I'm the daddy and you gonna talk to me like you got some sense."

She rolled her eyes. They were full of anger and sexual frustration. She would yell if she wanted to. But did he have to have this conversation on his knees in front of her bare yoni? Thank God she had the good sense to keep up with her intimate grooming.

Malik put his face at the entryway to her treasure, but he didn't put his mouth on her like she wanted. She squirmed in front of him, and the sight earned her a slow smile from Malik.

"Not until you tell me what I want to hear."

"No!"

Claudia was difficult as shit. Malik would get several things straight by the time the night was over. He stood and snatched at her bra until he figured out how to unhook it. She smirked up at him like she enjoyed his fumble.

He pulled her down to stand on those pretty feet and turned her around so she faced the counter. He donned the condom that he'd placed on the countertop and slapped her ass when she tried to turn and see. Claudia winced and moaned simultaneously.

"You like this shit, don't you?" He rested the tip of his stiffness at the entryway to her yoni but refused to move until she complied.

She nodded.

"Fuck no. I need you to use your mouth."

"OK." Claudia maneuvered herself so she faced Malik and dropped to a squat. With the condom still intact, she enveloped his manhood inside of her mouth. She followed his directions literally and used her mouth to dole out a little torture of her own.

"Oh, shit!" Malik yelled.

She licked and slurped but couldn't get at him the way she wanted. She released him and Malik thought he would die. The sexual torment he'd used on Claudia had backfired. He was desperate enough to hand over his company just to have another moment of her full lips around him again.

Before he could protest, she surprised him when she pulled the rubber off.

"Baby—"

"I can't taste you like I want," she said with the sexiest frustrated look on her face Malik had ever seen.

His toes curled. "OK, shit. You sure?"

She put her mouth around him and took him in like he belonged there. She lightly grazed her teeth against his length and his knees buckled.

"Got damn!"

Claudia had taken the driver's seat and was in total domination mode. She pulled her lips over her teeth and sucked Malik like he was a popsicle, for long moments. When he'd had enough of her intoxicating fellatio, he reached down and grasped her by the neck, pulling her to her feet.

"What you trying to do to me, Claudia Vaughn? You trying to get me to sign over the rights to my company?" Malik's words were playful, but he spoke them through gritted teeth and a contorted face.

Claudia laughed lightly—he was too damn cute. Malik flashed her an opened-mouth smile, showcasing the diamonds in his mouth that made her center drip.

"Turn around."

Without hesitation, she did as she was told.

Malik entered her savagely. "Am I hurting you?"

She nodded.

"You want me to stop?"

"Fuck, no!" Claudia cried out. "Don't stop, daddy, please."

And he didn't. Malik plowed into her repeatedly. Claudia's mouth had had an effect on him in more ways than one. But he allowed his strokes to serve as both a reward and a punishment for what she did with that pretty little mouth.

Claudia's sex sounds had Malik in a pussy fucking trance. Each one drove him to pummel her harder. He used his left hand to hold her steady at her hip, and the other was wrapped around the back of her neck. She intentionally clapped her ass like she was in one of those twerkouts Malik saw, and he considered he may have met his match.

"Hell yeah! I like that shit," he said through what sounded like a smirk to Claudia. His hand stung when he slapped her ass. The boisterous thud against her supple skin further aroused them both.

She turned her head to see the mischievous diamond studded grin on his handsome face. *Damn he's fine! But he's having* too *much fun.* Claudia grasped Malik's hand from her neck and pulled it to her face. She gave him one last backward glance before she took his pointer finger into her mouth.

Malik's eyes rolled upward. He continued with his strokes, but they'd lost the tenacity they had before his hand was nestled in her warm mouth. He had trouble deciding which sensation he preferred. Her tongue against his finger reminded him of how she'd licked his dick a few moments earlier. The area beneath his balls tingled like he was done for, but he willed himself to stay in a little longer.

Claudia sucked on Malik's finger like she had on the area between his legs. She hummed and moaned on it the way she'd wanted to while she was on her knees but wasn't given the chance.

"Which one is wetter?" Her voice was laced in seduction, and Malik wanted her to shut her pretty mouth so he could concentrate. At the rate she went, it wouldn't be long.

"Huh?"

"I asked you which was wetter, my pussy or my mouth?"

"Oh, shit!" Malik roared as he slammed into her one final time.

Malik's heavy frame rested on Claudia's back as they caught their breath.

"Damn, girl. You something else, you know that?"

Claudia craned her neck to meet his eyes. There seemed to be nothing that calmed her the way his authoritative voice and dick did. She shivered at the thought. Malik shifted his body, still connected to her, and laid his hoodie on her back.

"Are you cold?" he asked. He sounded exhausted.

"A little." She was cold, but her shiver had a lot more to do with the man than the temperature.

He reluctantly removed himself from her warmth and sauntered into a nearby bathroom. Claudia draped Malik's hoodie over her satiated body. She wasn't sure what type of entanglement she'd gotten herself into with Malik. In the past year—since her divorce was final—she'd found herself in a fling or two. But when she yelled at them or dismissed them, she expected them to disappear.

With Malik, her brain and her yoni were not on one accord. Other than his financial aspirations and his beautiful family, she didn't know shit about him. He'd bit her head off when she said she thought John John was his, so he didn't have kids. But what about a woman... or two with the way he'd satisfied her? Was Malik single?

Claudia's gut told her, his attention was on his business. But what if he'd made it up? She hadn't thought to do any internet stalking on him except for his employee status at Glamazon. She decided maybe she should be grateful Malik had been kind enough to share his magical dick with her after she'd gotten him fired.

Malik washed his hands in her spotless bathroom. Claudia must've had a maid along with her landscaper. He splashed water on his face. What the hell just happened? He was convinced Claudia had put some pussy hoodoo on him to get him to fuck her without a condom or verbal consent. He was surprised by his carelessness.

Because he'd been a celebrated athlete since he was in elementary, his dad sat him down for the talk, the summer before his freshman year. Malik assured his dad that they'd had the sex talk and the police talk already. He knew about condoms, crazy women, and how to behave appropriately around trigger-happy men who would mischaracterize him based on his size.

Robert Malone told him they needed to have one last talk before he started high school. Before they sat down, Malik didn't know shit about consent. He thought it was something he had to sign to play sports. His dad explained how the same concept applied to sex.

In a serious, matter-of-fact tone, his dad told him he was not to have sex with a girl who said no or said nothing at all. The girl was to give a verbal yes before he could sleep with her. At first, Malik complained it would make him sound corny if he asked for a girl's verbal permission. But Robert challenged him to make that shit 'swaggy' and make it work; otherwise, he could be accused of rape.

Of all the talks he had with his father, that was the one they had the most often. When he was off to college, his father educated him on the nuances of the gray area. The whole concept terrified Malik, so getting a 'yes' became his highest priority. Claudia had complied in the truck, but what if she changed her mind about what they'd done in the kitchen.

He blinked himself back into the present and dried his face with a paper towel. When he came out of the bathroom, Claudia was perched atop her countertop, legs opened, with only his hoodie on. Her provocative body language matched the energy in her eyes and the smirk on her lips. *Is she trying to go again? Already? Shit!*

"We need a safe word."

Claudia hopped down, and Malik released a breath. He couldn't focus when he could see her bare lips facing his direction. He shook his head as if it would clear the fog.

"How about Hood? Like your company," she asked once she was in front of him.

He lowered his eyes to meet hers, although her lips distracted him with the way she'd tucked the bottom one between her teeth. "How about something that doesn't turn me on."

She seemed to weigh his words. Claudia's smile widened as she offered, "Red."

He stiffened. "Yeah, that'll do it. There's nothing sexy about that damn snake."

"No? A lot of men think it's sexy to see a woman with a snake."

"Fuck them dudes."

"Are you seeing anyone?" Claudia blurted the question before she lost the nerve.

"Ain't that what we doin'?" He moved around her, butt naked. After all they'd done, the sight of Malik's ass still brought a blush to Claudia's cheeks.

"Are you seeing anybody *else*, Mr. Hood Body Briefs?"

He peeped around in her cabinets like he'd made himself at home. When he found a glass, he filled it with the filtered water from her upgraded refrigerator. He silently wondered why someone who rarely did anything besides work, would have access to the technology from a cook's wildest dreams. *Claudia probably can't boil water.* He turned to face her.

"I don't have time to be seeing your mean ass, let alone somebody else."

Satisfied with his response, she made her way to his side and unintentionally let a yawn escape her lips. He set his glass down and picked her up. Malik walked Claudia to her bedroom and pleased her one last time before they both settled into a restful sleep.

* * *

MALIK HAD AWAKENED at an ungodly hour and placed kisses to her face and eventually her breasts. When she wouldn't respond verbally to his questions, he put her toes in his mouth. That got her attention, because it was hard to ignore the moisture that pooled between her legs.

"I got shit I need to take care of."

"OK, bye," she fussed.

Since they were still naked, he pulled back the covers and bit her on the ass. The area on her backside stung, and she got his message loud and clear.

She propped herself on her hand and huffed, "Sorry. I don't want you to go, but I need more sleep. I don't talk in the morning."

"I bet if it was work, you'd talk to me," he teased.

She nodded and struggled to focus on his fully dressed appearance.

"I'll call you later, Ms. Hood Body Briefs."

"You're not my daddy," she said as she buried her head beneath a pillow.

He slapped her ass and relished the shake of her cheeks. "You'll pay for that later."

Nine

IT WAS FRIDAY, and Claudia had been able to find the resolve to focus on her work, despite her new distraction. Malik Malone was like a masculine turtle. His outer shell was ferocious, but he was gentle once he'd warmed up to her. The two of them were alike in that way. They hadn't seen each other since the weekend, but he texted or called her when he had time.

Claudia thought she worked a lot, but she didn't have shit on Malik's hustle. He'd pull a ten- or sometimes twelve-hour shift, making deliveries, and still made time to invest the little energy he had left on learning his craft. Claudia still hadn't spoken to Nick after the stunt he pulled, and he'd privately messaged her, asking if they could chat.

But she had non-work-related plans; Nick would have to wait. She'd gotten Malik to tell her where he was for lunch so she could pop up on him at the job. It was a risky move, but with each day they spoke, she could hear the exhaustion through the phone. While she respected his hustle, she was slightly worried he'd neglected himself.

He admitted he worked on aspects of the clothing line during his lunch and often didn't eat anything. She found the Jamaican restaurant he ordered last week on the internet and headed there from her home. If she'd timed it right, she could pick up the food and be at his job to see him, with thirty minutes to spare before his break was over. Malik may not have utilized his break to eat, but he took the full hour.

Claudia quickly changed into a dress she was certain Malik would love. She'd been obsessed with the color gray since as far back as she could remember. The color was mild but complemented her skin wonderfully. She'd reached in the back of her closet for her impromptu visit.

Claudia dressed with time to spare and rolled her eyes when she saw Nick's contact appear on the screen to her smartphone. She programmed the address to the restaurant into her car's virtual assistant and contemplated whether to face their first one-on-one call since his visit. The weather was nice, and she felt sexier than she had in quite a while.

She decided to quickly send a voice message response to Nick.

"Hey, Nick. I know you're ready to chat, but I need a little more time. I'd love to meet up on Monday and speak face to face, if that works for you. I'm going to be driving and away from my phone, so I may not see your response right away. Thank you for following up. See you soon."

As she made the drive from her home to the restaurant, she felt good about her decision to communicate with her mentor. She knew it needed to happen sooner rather than later, but she also knew herself. If she spoke to Nick and he pissed her off, she might not calm down by the time she arrived at Malik's job. He didn't deserve any other energy from her.

Malik warned her several times to speak to him respectfully. Part of her wanted to honor his request, and another part of her wanted to push him to the edge. Claudia was willing to take the punishment and anything else Malik Malone would dole out.

She entered the quaint Jamaican restaurant and felt a wave of familiarity. Claudia had never been to that side of town, but the way the people greeted her caused a moment of sadness to settle in her heart. The moment she entered, they asked her name and if she was there to dine in or pick up. She told them her name and was ushered to the bar until the food came out.

Why couldn't things be easy with her family? She missed them. She even missed her sister. She wondered if Victoria had started prep for the movie. Before she could talk herself out of it, she opened her phone and sent her twin a message.

Claudia: *Hey Vicky. I miss you. How are things going with the role?*

Claudia released a breath. She could only imagine what Victoria Vaughn would do with a vulnerable text like the one she'd just sent. It was one of the reasons Claudia was guarded around all of them except for JW.

Vicky: *Very funny*

Claudia: *I'm serious. I don't mean to make it awkward, but I don't want to keep asking JW how you are. Are you having fun with it?*

Vicky: *I'm so nervous I could poop a log*

Claudia: Crying laughing emoji *Don't tell mom, she'll lecture you for being an almost thirty yr old who says poop.*

Vicky: *Ugh, you're absolutely right. She's exhausting. Miss you too. I'm actually in a script meeting. Gotta go.*

Claudia was floored at the simple exchange she'd shared. She always texted with her brother in an effortless manner. They rarely talked in depth or at length, but they were close, nonetheless.

"Claudy?"

Claudia's body stiffened. She knew before she turned to face him who the voice belonged to.

Tommy Butner stood at her side dressed in a magenta polo and gray colored khaki shorts. He was as fit as he'd been in college and as handsome as the day she'd met him. The worry lines that adorned his forehead were new, but otherwise, he was Tommy Butner in the flesh.

Several of the women and staff had their eyes shamelessly locked on him. Claudia understood. The air in which he carried himself in college had been amplified from politician status to presidential. His swagger screamed 'man of importance', and his name and money fueled the flames.

"Hey," was all she could muster. She hadn't prepared to see him again outside of court. The fact that she hadn't jumped up and slapped him was probably thanks to Malik and all the fucking they'd done. A small smile broke across her face, despite her discomfort with Tommy's presence.

"You look great." Tommy's eyes raked across Claudia's body in a familiar way. She knew the look. It was the 'I'll pull a muscle trying to fuck you all night' look. Tommy and Claudia never had any issues in the bedroom. That was his problem. He liked to fuck, and he liked to fuck a lot.

But when things soured between them, they'd stopped fucking, but *he* hadn't.

"Thank you," Claudia said with her eyes and neck craned up to see him.

"Here's your jerk chicken with rice and peas, cabbage, and plantain. And your brown stew chicken with rice and peas, greens, and plantain," a beautiful young woman said sweetly as she handed Claudia her to-go order.

"Damn, that's a lot of food."

Claudia stood. She was proud that she hadn't gotten emotional over her first Tommy sighting. Malik said he ran into him; maybe he'd seen him there. She hadn't seen the bright diaper bag in his hand before, but it meant wife number two was likely near. Claudia wouldn't push her luck. She knew his family was beautiful, and the last thing she needed was to see a small child with his face and a happy woman wearing his ring.

"It was nice seeing you," Claudia said as she gathered the food.

"Wait... Are you seeing somebody?"

She felt her blood boil. It didn't take much to get her started.

"What?"

"Sounds like you ordered food for you and another person."

"And what if I did? It's none of your fucking..." She looked around and realized they had a small audience. "It's none of your fucking business," she whisper yelled.

"There's the Claudy I know."

She shoulder checked him as she walked by.

"Go fuck yourself."

He grabbed her by the arm to hold her in place.

"You tell whoever he is, you belong to me and always will, Mrs. Butner." Tommy maintained his tight grip on her arm as he spoke, and the hairs on Claudia's neck stood up.

Meanwhile, they both looked up to find Tommy's wife and toddler at the entryway of the restaurant. The walls seemed to close in on Claudia. She knew his wife and child were stunning. They looked like they belonged on television. She recalled how bold the woman had been when she approached Claudia at the cafe two years ago. And now they were married with a child and another on the way.

Claudia snatched away from him and held her head high as she exited the restaurant, aware that everyone, including the Butners, watched as she did.

* * *

CLAUDIA SAT OUTSIDE in the parking lot of Malik's work for several minutes, before she found the strength to get out. Her mind wandered and fought to determine how to process the old ghosts from her past.

What the hell just happened? She'd freshened up her makeup and tried to look like she hadn't been crying. She'd been tempted to drive home but thought that would be like letting Tommy win. *How the hell could he put his hands on me? I should've punched him!* It was the menacing way he'd spoken that gave her pause.

She adjusted her clothes and checked her watch. She stepped into the lobby of Postbuddies with twenty-five minutes left on Malik's lunch break. Claudia looked past the interested glares and cat calls she received from the workers, because she was on a mission. She needed to be around Malik's energy more than ever.

"How can I help you?" a bald man who'd about lost his balance in his attempt to stand and greet Claudia asked.

She saw him scrolling on his phone before she caught his attention. The truth was, she needed help to find the business office. It was where Malik mentioned he spent his lunch breaks.

"I'm looking for the business office. Bringing lunch to one of your employees." Claudia lifted the bag of Jamaican food to plead her case.

"Malone's the only one who uses it."

Claudia smiled brightly, and realization covered his pale cheeks. "You're here for Malone?"

"Yes, sir."

"I'll escort you there myself. I'm Norman, by the way."

"Nice to meet you."

They walked the dense hallway, as Norman's eyes bounced between her legs and her face. It seemed to be his attempt to be on his best behavior, but from what she could see, there simply wasn't enough feminine energy in the building.

"You have a guest, Malone," Norman said in a raspy voice once they entered the surprisingly quiet business office. It was a spacious oasis that was a stark contrast to the chaotic action on the other side of the wall.

"I'm busy, Norman. As soon as my break is up, I'll deliver all the food." Malik's voice was full of sarcasm, and it still sent shivers up her spine. It didn't matter what Malik said, her body responded. She wondered if they could have each other for lunch in lieu of the food.

"I don't mind spending time with an attractive woman with a killer pair of legs and a meal that smells almost as good as she does," he responded to Malik. "No offense," he added for Claudia.

Her light giggle was what made Malik finally tear his eyes from his opened laptop and book. He'd taken notes in a notebook, like he'd been consumed by his work.

Claudia stepped inside of the office and lifted the bag again. "I brought food."

"You two, have fun." Norman guffawed and closed the door behind him. Claudia could still hear his taunting laughter through the sealed barrier.

In the short time she'd known Malik, she'd never known him to wear glasses. It was a pleasant surprise and another sensual contrast to his street style and persona. Malik's frames were dark and only covered the top of his lenses. The clear portion at the bottom put her in the mind of the infamous Malcolm X photos. He looked good enough to eat.

"I must be dreamin'," Malik said in an unhurried cadence.

"And why is that?"

"Well, imagine my surprise when I thought to myself how I'm hungry as shit, but I wouldn't have time to get something worth eating and get at this." He pointed to his work, and Claudia was convinced she'd fallen in love.

His commitment to his dream had him unfed, and it was a need she could meet.

She set the to-go bag of food on an empty table near him and found a sink to wash her hands. She could feel the heat of Malik's gaze escort her ass around the space.

"Are you serious?" he asked when she bent over to grab the napkin she dropped. The dress rode up enough to get him frazzled. He closed the distance between them and was next to her ear when he whispered, "I don't give a shit about this job, Claudia. I'll fuck you right here."

She used her hand to stroke the side of his jaw where a thin line of facial hair outlined his chiseled features.

He tugged at the side of her hood. "You came here to torture me, wearing this shit."

"I didn't. I knew you would like it, but I also knew you wouldn't eat during your *lunch* break."

He regarded her silently for so long, she wondered if she'd done too much.

"You don't like it?"

He pulled her to him and gave her the tightest hug. She thanked God she hadn't let her run-in with Tommy's psycho ass keep her from Malik.

He lifted her chin and kissed her leisurely.

When she pulled back, he pulled his lips into his mouth and licked them.

"Damn, you taste good."

They sat and talked about what he worked on for Hood Body Briefs. He'd thoroughly identified his target audience and the best locations to sell his product. He'd even discussed a few buy-out offers that they both agreed were trash.

"Enough about me. Thank you for the food."

"You're welcome."

"I already said I ain't seein' nobody else."

"I know."

He eyed her cautiously. "This some heavy on the girlfriend type shit."

She shrugged her shoulders. "Too much, too soon?"

"Hell nah." Malik stretched his long legs across the table where they were seated face to face. His legs were on either side of hers. "How's your day? Nick fuckin' with you on the job?"

She let out a loud sigh. "No, but he did reach out twice. I finally told him I would be up for a conversation on Monday."

Malik asked for her benefit only. He wouldn't waste another moment of his time with Claudia on old balls Nick. "You look pretty as hell, but you also look a little... sad."

Claudia swallowed. There went her appetite. Tommy Butner had that effect on her. She'd been living her best life, and then a mention or sighting of him would punch her in the gut.

"When I picked up the food, I ran into my ex." Claudia's entire mood shifted. Her eyes were downcast and mindlessly focused on her rice and peas.

"Are you OK?"

"Yeah. He came at me kind of crazy, but I froze when he felt the need to touch me."

"Claudia."

She lifted her head to face him, and the concern in his eyes made her heart beat triple time.

"He put his hands on you?"

The fact that Malik hadn't raised his voice made her afraid... for Tommy.

"He grabbed me, but I..."

Malik closed his eyes and steadied his breath. *What the fuck is Butner's problem? He has a pregnant second wife, and he's still not satisfied?*

"How?"

Claudia bit nervously on her bottom lip. "How what?"

"How did he put his hands on you? Did he grab you like I grab you?"

"No. I mean, yes."

Malik stood and paced the business office. She looked at her watch to see he only had about fifteen minutes left in his break.

"It's not that you grab me too tightly; it's just I know we're gonna fuck right after." Claudia didn't miss the almost smile on Malik's handsome face. "It was nothing sexual with Tommy, at least on my side. It was intimidation, I suppose. He asked if I was seeing someone when he heard my order read aloud by the hostess."

Claudia stood and walked to where Malik stood fuming.

"He feeds off attention. I don't want to waste any more of our time on him."

Malik leaned in and kissed her gently. "I hear you. But hear me... If he ever even fixes his lips to say an unkind word to you, my waistband friend is gonna have some words for him. You understand what I mean?"

She nodded. "And he'd deserve it, but you don't."

Malik started to object, but she covered his mouth with her hand.

"We only have a little time left. What do you want to do with me?"

Malik's eyes perked up. "Claudia Vaughn, you so damn nasty. You know exactly what I wanna do."

She stared at him blankly as if his flirtatious innuendos didn't faze her at all.

He grabbed her hand and led her to a vacant room within the business office. They spent the last ten minutes of Malik's break in a muted version of their truck and kitchen ritual.

Ten

MALIK AND CLAUDIA made plans to get together over the weekend, but his sister needed help with John John. He offered for her to hang out for a while, but Claudia was deathly afraid of children.

She didn't feel like she had a maternal bone in her body. Victoria, however, couldn't wait to be a mother. It was one of the reasons Claudia believed she did so well with her voice over assignments; most of them were content created for children.

She hadn't told Malik about her fears. She simply lied about needing to attend to work, when, in reality, Claudia could do her work with her eyes closed. She'd received several compliments from her boss on how relaxed she was lately. She would be sure to thank Malik for that when she saw him again.

It was early afternoon on a Monday, and Claudia wasn't overly concerned with her to-do lists. She was still productive, but a hell of a lot less stressed. She wore casual clothes that were appropriate for online work calls, but certainly not work attire.

The ringing of her phone snapped her back to reality. *Shit! I forgot about Nick.* Claudia had made plans to meet him at a cafe in twenty minutes, but it slipped her mind.

If she left in five minutes, she'd get there on time. She didn't bother changing out of her multicolor printed belt dress. The length and cut were appropriate, but the split was a bit risky for a work brunch. Claudia shrugged her shoulders as if to respond to her own hesitation. This was the beauty of a work from home gig.

Claudia grabbed her phone and bag as she hustled to her car. She rushed through the back roads with her sensual music louder than usual. She felt like Malik had influenced her to loosen up, and she loved every change as a result.

The valet flashed Claudia a charmed smile as he took her key and exchanged it for a ticket. She adjusted her dress and removed her sunglasses as she entered the brunch bar Nick suggested. Claudia felt like it was an establishment her mother would have chosen. For the Vaughns to be free people, they certainly didn't mind the company of the ridiculously bourgeois.

The hostess didn't lift her gaze to meet Claudia's. She simply bit out, "We're only taking reservations at this time. No walk-ins."

"Great. I'm here to see Nicholas Westfield."

The young girl's head flew up, and her eyes widened. She regarded Claudia wordlessly.

"Is he here already?"

Claudia checked her watch and found it was five minutes after their scheduled meeting time. It wasn't like Nick to be late.

"Yes. He's waiting for you in a private area on the patio," a male hostess said and motioned for her to follow him. He scowled at the other hostess, who seemed in a daze.

Claudia followed the employee, unbothered by the girl's hesitation. She didn't know if it was because she was black or because the girl may have had a thing for Nick, but she wouldn't waste her time worrying about it. With the good dick Malik delivered to Claudia regularly, there was very little that could ruin her mood.

Nick stood dressed impeccably. He had not come from wealth but was one of those people who did everything in his power to shift the paradigm for himself and those he loved. It cost him his marriage, and he'd just started the process to repair his relationship with his adult children.

They'd gotten closer in the past two years while Claudia had gone through a painful separation of her own. He'd been a sounding board on the days she couldn't bring herself to concentrate on work. Nick understood how it felt to need to be one hundred percent on the job while your personal life was in shambles.

Now she wondered if maybe boundaries had been crossed and lines blurred because of the details she'd shared. He was her shoulder to cry on and her motivation to excel in her career. Had he gotten the wrong impression?

"You look splendid, Claudy," Nick said as he stood and kissed her cheek. The host gave her a polite nod, then stepped away.

Suddenly, Nick's actions didn't feel harmless. *Has he always been this way? Or is Malik making me paranoid?*

"Thank you."

"I ordered a mimosa for you. I hope that was OK."

Claudia wouldn't drink during brunch. She wanted a clear head while she figured out if her relationship with her mentor was salvageable.

"I'm good for now. Thanks, though."

She sat and faced him as if she could find the answers she needed without words.

"I want to start by apologizing for last week. What I pulled with Red was unacceptable."

Claudia nodded.

"I've never seen you as carefree as you were with him, and I guess I just don't want to see you hurt or making any bad decisions."

Claudia tried not to take his concern personally. Had she or Malik given him any reason to believe she was incapable of taking care of herself? Then she remembered how harshly she'd judged Malik. She got the man fired because he didn't behave in the way she felt he should. Of course, Nick would have concerns.

"When you say bad decisions, do you mean because I'm dating or because of who I'm dating?"

Nick choked on his water. He had such a hard time that a waiter appeared at his side to offer his assistance, but Nick waived him off vehemently. It took everything Claudia had in her not to laugh. Maybe Malik had been right all along.

"You're dating... *him*?" Nick wore confusion across his proud face.

"Yes, Nick. We're dating. I know it seems unconventional, because we're certainly from two different worlds, but he's kind, he's protective, and incredibly driven. Malik is everything I need after all I went through with Tommy." Her stomach dropped at the mention of Tommy. She'd replayed his words—and reimagined the icy look he had—since their last run-in, and each time, it made her edgy.

Nick took a gulp of a clear liquor she didn't recognize. "I'm shocked. I thought maybe it was a casual thing."

"I'm going to cut in before the conversation gets any more personal than it already has. I don't want you to get the impression that I'm seeking your validation in any way. I'm looking for more clarity on why you felt the need to behave the way you did and to ensure we can move forward professionally."

Nick regarded Claudia for long moments. They'd had an amazing personal and professional relationship, and she hoped he wouldn't let his pride ruin it.

"I respect what you're saying. And again, I apologize for overstepping. I think you're a fantastic woman, and you have barely scratched the surface of your potential. I'd like to continue to serve as your mentor, if you'll have me."

Claudia allowed his words to settle over her before she scrunched up her face playfully. "I guess I'll keep you."

Nick's laughter boomed. He hadn't distracted anyone, since they were seated away from most of the other patrons.

"With that said, how are things with work?"

"They're good. I thought the promotion would mean more work, but if I'm honest, it's been easy."

Nick gave her a big smile. "You'll find that the hard work you've done will serve as a sort of investment. It's not that you'll do less work, but it will become less and less taxing."

Since they were on the topic of working less, Claudia remembered a good friend of Nick's who left the company to pursue investing full time.

"Do you still keep in touch with Richard?"

"I'm meeting him today for a late round of golf. Why?"

"I have a company he might be interested in." Claudia couldn't be sure if Malik would be comfortable with her seeking investor information via Nick, but she couldn't resist.

"Tell me about the company."

* * *

MALIK MISSED Claudia over the weekend. He hadn't been in a long-term relationship since college, so the sentiment was foreign. He'd missed a woman's pussy before, but not the woman. If he was honest, he missed her sassy mouth and her wet ass pussy. After he delivered food to a woman who tried to get him to come inside, he really wanted to see Claudia.

It was Monday, and he had a gang of shit to do, but she was a welcomed distraction. He perched himself against his truck in the parking lot of a gas station and requested a video call. She accepted the call, and her flawless face made his pants tighten and his heart swell.

"Hey," Claudia said sweetly.

"Hey, yourself. You look pretty."

"Damn, I must be bad to get a country boy like you to say that."

Malik twisted his face up. "Here you go with this. Where you at?"

"I'm finishing brunch with Nick."

Malik sat with his eyes focused on his screen. He wasn't threatened by Nick, but he was annoyed that he wanted to fuck Claudia.

"OK. I wanna see you," Malik said unashamed because it was the truth.

"When?"

"Call me when you're done with work. Maybe we can do something tonight or tomorrow." Malik didn't have the day off, but if she said yes, he would take one.

"Sounds like a plan, daddy." Claudia's devilish grin was unwavering.

Malik swallowed and looked around to see if anyone could hear his conversation. "I thought you said you were at brunch."

She lifted her phone and flipped her camera. Nick had his eyes on anything but Claudia as she took her call, but it was apparent he could hear her flirting.

"You're something else," Malik said once she returned the camera toward her face.

"I know. I'll speak to you soon."

Malik disconnected the call and finished his shift with renewed energy and motivation. Claudia was going to fuck around and have him whipped if she kept it up.

Once his shift was over, he texted her from his parents' house.

Malik: *I want to take you somewhere*

Pretty ass Claudia: *yes*

Malik: *You're not going to ask where*

Pretty ass Claudia: *nope. Do I sound thirsty?* Embarrassed face emoji

Malik: *You sound wet* purple devil emoji

Pretty ass Claudia: *Maybe I am. Where are you taking me?*

Malik: *Camping*

Pretty ass Claudia: *Have you met me?*

Malik: *Yes, and that's exactly why I want you with me when I go.*

Pretty ass Claudia: *Fine*

Malik: *Lol, don't overdo it. Just bring a sleeping bag, a blanket, toiletries, and a change of clothes.*

Pretty ass Claudia: *I can't believe you want me to go camping. When?*

Malik: *I sure do. Tomorrow night.*

Pretty ass Claudia: *You better make it worth my while*

Malik: *Don't worry. After tomorrow, you'll never look at camping the same*

Pretty ass Claudia: *I'm going to sleep. Goodnight... Daddy*

Malik: *You gonna send me to bed with a hard dick*

Pretty ass Claudia: Wink face emoji

* * *

THE NEXT DAY, Claudia was distracted during her work meetings. Luckily, she wasn't involved with any solo projects because she spent the majority of the day and most of the afternoon making orders to local shops for her camping trip. Malik told her not to go overboard, but after their hike, she wanted to be prepared.

She ordered a popup tent that could be assembled and taken down with the press of a button. She'd ordered those big candles with bug repellant in the wick. Along with her sleeping bag, she ordered a hammock because she'd never been in one before. A large area of her foyer was crammed with her camping trip items.

Claudia ordered extra hand sanitizer, disinfectant wipes, and all sorts of dry food and snacks. She packed three sets of outfits and underwear—both functional and a few for Malik's enjoyment. She had a flashlight and a portable umbrella in case there was an unexpected storm. This time, Claudia would be ready. She bought the cutest pair of hiking boots she could find.

Overwhelmed by her work and planning, Claudia lay down for a quick nap. She wanted to be rested when Malik arrived. She'd intended to set an alarm for twenty minutes but fell asleep before she had the chance.

Loud knocks to her door pulled her from her sleep and notified her that her hip prince charming had arrived. She stood and rushed to a mirror to freshen up. She fluffed the back of her natural hair where she'd rested it against the couch and blew into her palm to ensure her breath was fresh.

Her fitted jacket hugged her just right. Her pants were loose fitting and hung from her waist to the top of her boots. She was covered from head to toe. His knocks sounded again, and when she saw the screen of her phone, she knew why. Malik had called her twice already.

She swung the door open to see a fine yet concerned Malik.

"Hey," she greeted him sweetly. "I fell asleep."

Malik's concerned face was replaced with one of amusement as he took in her attire. "Baby, what are you wearing?"

Claudia's arms crossed in front of her chest, and anger rose within her body. "Fucking hiking clothes. What does it look like?" She stomped her foot, unable to conceal her tantrum.

"I swear you trying to get out of this trip talking to me crazy. I'm not fucking you before we leave, so can you calm your ass down." Malik did his best to hide his smile. She wasn't slick. She knew what talking like that would get her, but he also got the impression she didn't really want to hike.

"What's wrong with what I'm wearing?"

"I said I'm taking you camping."

"People hike to campgrounds all the time." Claudia rolled her eyes to the heavens. What was with this man and making fun of her?

"You're right. Let me get your bag." Malik stepped in and burst into laughter when he saw the corner and all she'd purchased.

"I told you not to go overboard."

She smiled up at him and shrugged her shoulders. "I've never been camping, and you pointed out how ill prepared I was for the hike. I just wanted to have everything I needed."

Malik started his own pile alongside hers.

"What are you doing?" she whined.

"I'm taking out the things you don't need."

"You took out the tent!"

He turned his body to face her. He ambled in her direction and leaned in inches from her lips. "You trust me?"

She nodded, although the pout remained on her lips.

"OK. You don't need this much stuff. I promise." He smiled down at her, and the ice in his mouth melted her anger as quickly as it came.

Malik grabbed a third of all that Claudia purchased and loaded it into his trunk. Once they were buckled in, she leaned over and placed a kiss on his cheek.

"What was that for? I thought you were pissed because I didn't bring your hammock or the mosquito net," Malik teased.

Claudia kissed her teeth. "Don't make me take my kiss back." She rolled her eyes and crossed her arms across her chest. But Malik grabbed one of her hands and held it as he drove.

Claudia watched their small town get more rural as he drove twenty-five minutes south. They weren't near any woods. The only thing Claudia saw were plots of land. Some were new builds, while others were still under construction. Malik entered a housing division with a sign that detailed it would be built within the next two years.

He weaved through the soon-to-be neighborhood like he'd been there before. She was once again confused by his actions, but he was right; she trusted him.

"This is it."

Claudia craned her neck to look around. There was a massive unfinished home in front of them with the wood exposed. It reminded her of a science project she helped JW with where he had the bright idea to build a replica of their home from popsicle sticks. Slabs of wood and various construction materials were near what would eventually become the front entrance.

"This is what?"

"Where I'm taking you. Get out." Malik had his signature panty dropping grin across his face, the one that had Claudia on a hike and now on some kind of camping trip.

They closed the doors and leaned on the passenger side of his car to look at the home.

"This is my house."

Claudia's breath caught. This was easily a seven-hundred-thousand-dollar home.

"It's not exactly camping. Maybe I should have asked if you would dream with me."

She looked up at him in pure adoration.

"I stay here whenever I need the extra motivation to keep going. Security knows me because I didn't want to get arrested for squatting."

They shared a quiet laugh. Claudia's eyes misted as he continued.

"I wanted to share this part of my dream with you too."

"I don't know what to say."

He wrapped his arm around her neck and pulled her into his side as he kissed her forehead. "Say you'll return the tent and all that other shit."

She pushed him as they shared more laughter. Claudia wasn't sure when it happened, but she'd caught feelings for Malik Malone. She hoped she wouldn't come to regret it.

Eleven

MALIK'S HOME WAS MAGNIFICENT. He pulled out the architectural plans and laid them down to show her what would go where. As he spoke in his southern and unhurried cadence, Claudia held on to his every word. He told her how he had another year before interest would be added to his payments.

He'd taken the home construction loan as a motivator to do whatever needed to be done with his business within the strict time frame.

"I meant to tell you I found a new manufacturer for Hood Body Briefs. The last one had ridiculously long turnaround times and didn't disclose the additional shipping costs. This one is clear and super-efficient—like your ass."

Claudia gaped at him.

"Why you lookin' at me like that, Ms. Vaughn?" He'd barely taken a breath. He was so excited to share the details with someone he cared about. Malik would finally admit he cared for Claudia, no matter how long it'd been since he knew her.

"I think I'm in love..." her eyes were bright and playful, "...with your hustle."

"Is that right?" He gazed down at her, then tugged on her coat. "I love your sass and this ass."

They kissed, and Claudia felt the walls around her heart dissolve. Tommy had treated her horribly, yet her brain couldn't accept it because of who he was. She'd gaslighted herself to think he was a good man and therefore could do no wrong. For the first time in two years, she thanked God for her divorce. Without it, she never would have met Mr. Hood Body Briefs himself.

* * *

ONCE THE SUN had gone down, Claudia understood why Malik said they'd be camping. If she needed to use the bathroom, they'd have to walk to a row of port-a-potties at the far end of the street. Malik's hiking lantern made his home feel like a cabin. Though he talked her out of the majority of the items she ordered for their overnight trip, Claudia insisted on her battery powered heated blanket.

If there was any doubt in her mind that she loved Malik, it was gone when he presented a picnic basket with her favorite order from the Jamaican restaurant. Brown stew chicken and Malik was all she had an appetite for these days.

"I think we need to christen your place," she said as they lay on their stacked sleeping bags and blankets. She insisted they make a palate so they'd be more comfortable, and they could share her heating blanket to sleep under.

"How you wanna do that, baby?"

He knew what it did to her when he said baby like that.

"We fuck in every room."

Malik's eyes got wide. "Damn, you nasty, and I fuckin' love that shit!" He pulled Claudia on top of him, and she went willingly. She'd just bent down and shoved her tongue in his throat when Malik's phone buzzed.

The house was empty, except for the two of them and their overnight things, so the two of them heard the sound of his phone echo throughout the hollow space right away.

Claudia moved to separate them, but Malik urged her not to.

"Don't stop, baby, please. Fuck that phone," he whined.

"It might be important. It is the middle of the work week."

He mumbled a curse as she climbed off him.

"This shit better be important!" Malik barked into his phone.

Claudia was still close enough that she could hear Markita. "What's wrong? Is he OK?... Fuck. How long ago was he supposed to be home?" Malik's eyes went pained as he told his sister he'd be there soon and ended the call.

"Do you need to go?"

"Yeah, I do. John was supposed to drop John John off after preschool today."

"Oh my God." Claudia gasped. It was almost nine in the evening.

"I don't want to put you in the middle of my shit again. I need to take you home."

"Hell no."

Malik eyed her with confusion etched across his handsome face. "Baby—"

"I'm going with you." Claudia stood and fished around for her boots. She had on a skimpy dusty pink, matching sleep set. It was delicate and trimmed in lace, and Malik was positive she didn't have shit on underneath it.

"Put on clothes this time, shit!"

They both stared at each other with intensity. Neither of them wanted to back down, and both seemed to pop off at the drop of a hat.

Claudia grabbed a pair of pants and Malik's oversized T-shirt and dressed in record timing. He'd been so focused on her ass that he still didn't have on shoes.

"Hurry up, babe."

Malik hustled, and despite Claudia's refusal to let him drop her off at home, the two of them were in his car in less than five minutes. Their stuff would be fine. He needed to get to Markita and figure out what the hell happened with his nephew.

"What's the plan?" Claudia asked once they were en route.

"I'm going to check on my sister."

Claudia didn't respond. Instead, she focused on the road.

"OK, Bonnie. Since you're my rider all of a sudden, what do you suggest?"

Claudia could hear the irritation in Malik's voice, but she was positive it had nothing to do with her. If she knew Malik like she thought she did, he silently cursed himself for not killing John when he had the opportunity.

"Shouldn't we just go to John's and pick up your nephew?"

She's right. Of course, we should! Malik used his turn signal and made an illegal U-turn. *There is nothing sexier than a woman who has my back.* If he wasn't focused on John John, he would have pulled over and let Claudia ride him on the side of the road like she'd started in his unfinished home.

They were at John's house within fifteen minutes. His neighborhood was nothing like the area where Malik and Markita lived. Claudia briefly wondered if maybe, this time, she was in over her head.

Loose dogs walked the streets like they were on patrol. Several houses had cars parked out front that looked like they'd been abandoned and needed to be towed.

Claudia tried to play it cool, but small groups of people were scattered on different parts of the block—some were children. Whatever they were up to, it didn't seem like she had any business there. But she trusted that she was safe with Malik. *Damn, I love him!*

"That's it right there," Malik said as he nodded toward a home with one of those groups of people on the porch engrossed in a game of dice. Malik had his head on a swivel as he debated how safe it would be to leave Claudia in the car. Maybe he hadn't thought this through.

"Baby." she reached over and grasped his arm. "Your windows are tinted. Lock me in. Plus, I have my phone."

Malik's jaw clenched as he debated what to do next. "OK. But this time, if something don't seem right, call the police."

"I will."

Claudia leaned her seat back, and though the situation was anything but funny, it brought a half smile to Malik's face. *What movie she been watchin' where this is a practical way to stay alive? She cute as shit, but I can still see her titties.*

Malik strolled up to the steps, and Claudia recognized John as he stood to his full height. She cracked the window to hear the exchange between them in case she needed to call 9-1-1.

An old school car with a louder speaker than Malik's and tinted windows pulled up and parked in the driveway beside Malik. Claudia internally panicked. Why had she suggested they come here?

An older woman exited the car and eyed Malik curiously. "You must be Kita's kin. You look just like her!" she yelled. The woman was loud and could be heard over the outdoor chaos.

"Yes, ma'am. She's my twin, and John John is my nephew. Kita was expecting John John after preschool but couldn't get ahold of John."

John made his way to the two of them and joined the conversation. "He said he wanted to stay here tonight, Mama." John didn't seem much like a threat anymore—he seemed like a grown ass child cowering in his mother's presence.

"Since when you letting a child make decisions?"

John shrugged.

"Did you tell his mother you was keeping him here?"

"He sleep."

"Did I ask you if he was sleep? I asked if you told Kita where her baby was? I swear to God I woulda shot your raggedy ass daddy if he would've pulled some shit like that. Is you crazy?"

"Mama—"

"Don't 'mama' me. You must be crazy or stupid, if you can't see this man here to do some damage because his sister can't find her child. Go get John John."

"He sleep."

"I swear to God, I'mma slap yo' ass you tell me that baby sleep one more got damn time. Go get him and give him to his uncle!"

John's shoulders sank, but he did what his mom asked. Claudia could see Malik barely able to hold onto his laughter.

Moments later, John appeared at the door with a fully awake John John.

"Uncle Mayeek!"

"And come get these groceries out my car, boy."

Claudia released a breath as Malik thanked John's mother and carried his nephew to the car. She knew that was the best possible outcome, and things could have gone much worse.

* * *

CLAUDIA THOUGHT her parents had kept themselves in shape, but when she laid eyes on Robert and Angela Malone, she understood where Malik got his good looks.

"Mama, this is Claudia Vaughn," Malik said with pride.

Claudia slipped from his embrace and held out her hand to formally introduce herself.

Angela crossed her arms over her chest and asked, "You're the one who got my baby fired?"

"Mama—"

She held up her hand to her son and steadied her breath. Robert, Markita, and John John were as shocked as Claudia. His mother looked livid. She walked closer to where Claudia stood and leaned in and hugged her.

Everyone burst into laughter.

"I'm sorry. I had to give you a hard time. I told Malik you did him a favor. It's high time he left those taxing jobs and focus on the one he loves."

Claudia relaxed as his mother and father divulged how they'd never met one of Malik's girlfriends. Robert was impressed with the position she held with her company. It stung a bit when he said her parents must be proud. Malik had the type of family Claudia dreamed of; she loved that for him.

Claudia sat on Robert and Angela Malone's couch fully dressed this time. Just as she suspected, his family was full of love and acceptance. They were naturally inclusive people who welcomed Claudia in because of their deep desire to support Malik.

She couldn't spend much time with them, as they were headed to bed, but they insisted she come by one weekend when Malik wasn't busy with work.

It was John John's bedtime, and although Claudia had been able to avoid one-on-one contact with him, it was time to face her fears. Markita and Malik were both within eyeshot but preoccupied with other tasks.

"What's yo' name?" John John asked. He had his same blanket clutched in his sticky hands. Though Claudia found him undeniably adorable, she knew his hands and his blanket must have been covered in germs.

Not only was Claudia standoffish with children, but she was also a bit of a germaphobe.

"Claudia," she said with an even tone. Sweat beaded on her forehead, and she hoped children couldn't smell fear like animals.

"Why?" John John hadn't broken eye contact, though Claudia tried to get both Markita and Malik's attention to save her.

"My mom picked it."

"Why?"

"Wow. You sure ask a lot of questions." Claudia laughed uncomfortably. "She must have liked it."

"Why?" Each of his questions were at varied inflections as though he truly wanted an answer.

"OK, John John. It's time for bed," Markita said.

Claudia silently thanked God. She wasn't sure how long she could keep up his game before she got pissed. While Malik and Markita discussed who would put him to bed, Claudia quickly texted her sister. Although they'd only recently texted when Claudia asked about her new role, she knew Vicky was like a baby whisperer. If anyone would know what to do, it would be Victoria Vaughn.

CLAUDIA: *A guy I'm seeing has a nephew he adores. What do I do?*

Vicky: *LOL, you hate kids*

Claudia: *I know. I mean the kid is cute, but he looks sticky*

Vicky: *Claudy, that's because he probably is. Try to be patient with him*

Claudia: *huh? Have you met me?*

Vicky: *Unfortunately, I have. *Eye roll emoji Just treat the kid like you would treat Red, if she were sick*

Claudia: *I think it has to go to bed*

Vicky: *CLAUDY, it's a child, not an it *crying laughing emoji*

Claudia: *Oops, you're right. Thank you, Vicky*

Vicky: *It's my pleasure, Sis*

. . .

CLAUDIA COULDN'T HIDE her smile at the sight of her sister's text messages. She'd longed for a relationship with Victoria and hoped her responsiveness might be an indication of a shift in their relationship. Vicky was evil, but Claudia could admit she was a bitch. Maybe there was middle ground.

"What's that about?" Malik asked as Markita attempted to gather John John.

"I texted Vicky and told her I was afraid of your nephew," she whispered.

Malik laughed loudly. "Kita and I figured you must not do kids from the way you sat there like he was going to bite you."

"John John's biting phase ended almost two years ago," Kita added from the kitchen.

Panic covered Claudia's face. *What the hell?*

"That's exactly how I feel about your snake," Malik added. "What did your sister say?"

"She said to treat John John like I would treat Red if she were sick."

"Maybe there's hope for the evil twin after all."

"Who has a twin?" Markita returned to the living room where Claudia and Malik sat, with John John tucked under her arm like a load of laundry. He seemed content with his body flailing playfully.

"I do. I have a fraternal twin sister, but we aren't as tight as you two."

"Oh, no."

"It's been that way for years, but recently, it seems like it might get better. I'm not going to hold my breath, but I'm open."

Claudia's phone buzzed again.

Vicky: *Invite them to Dad's birthday party this weekend. I want to meet him... and his sticky nephew* *tongue out laughing emoji

"DO YOU WANNA MEET VICKY?" Claudia held her breath. She wasn't sure if this was the appropriate time to introduce him to her family. Besides, they were nowhere near as functional as his family seemed to be.

"I can't fuckin' wait." Malik leaned down and kissed her lips.

"Yuck!" John John shrieked.

Markita patted him lightly on his bottom, which earned her a thunderous toot. "Ugh, you so much like your uncle, it's ridiculous."

"Can they come too? Vicky wants to meet all of you at my dad's sixtieth birthday party."

"I don't mind, if they want to come. I know you can hear us, Kita. You wanna bring John John to a party with Claudia's twin and her family?"

"Yaaaaas!" Kita threw her hands in the air and whirled John John around. "I need an excuse to get out and do something fun."

"Let me take him and put him to bed," Malik said as he stood and took John John from Markita's arms. He turned and winked at Claudia, then disappeared down the hallway.

Kita took a seat across from Claudia and jumped right into conversation like they were old friends. "My brother really likes you."

Claudia blushed. She knew Malik cared for her, but to hear it from his sister—the person he was closest to—meant everything to her. "I like him too."

"I can tell. He told me it was your idea to go to John's." Kita's eyes looked distant, though her beautiful face sparkled like she didn't have a care in the world.

"When?"

"When you first got here. We have muted conversations all the damn time. It used to drive my parents nuts. I asked why he went to John's, and he nodded at you. I knew that meant it was your idea."

"Oh."

"Thank you." Kita walked over to the couch where Claudia sat. She leaned down and hugged her. Although Claudia was caught off guard, she happily accepted it.

"Are you OK?" Claudia shifted her position and tucked a leg under her so the two of them were face to face on the sofa. She hoped she could build a bond like this with her sister someday.

"Ugh. I think John is pissed after our conversation earlier. I went to the hospital after that night."

Claudia nodded. She remembered how Malik had almost used his waistband buddy on John.

"The hospital strongly encouraged me to file a police report. I told them John was my child's father, but a nurse pulled me aside and said it was all the more reason to do it. If any drama were to happen with custody, I would have a paper trail of his unstable behavior." Tears filled Kita's eyes as she spoke.

Claudia gave Markita her full attention and listened intently. It seemed all Kita needed was an adult's listening ear. Unfortunately, her twin couldn't hold space for her. He'd want to avenge her despite the nuance of the situation. It was complicated, because John was her son's father. And until he proved himself unfit as a dad, it appeared Kita would keep him in the picture.

"The police wanted to ask him questions about the incident, and when he asked if I'd reported him, I told him I had to. I think he kept John John to scare me."

"That's awful, Kita. How the hell did he pull you anyway?" Claudia asked. It was her version of the same anger everyone had whenever they learned of John's toxic behavior.

Markita sat quietly, then erupted into a fit of laughter. "I see why Malik likes you!"

Twelve

WHEN MALIK and Claudia left his parents' home a few nights ago, she felt like they were an actual couple after all they'd experienced together. They hadn't verbally made things official, but he showed her in all the ways that mattered. Malik apologized that their romantic evening at his unfinished home was cut short, and Claudia admitted she preferred to sleep in a bed with him.

She filled him in on her conversation with Markita, and he later updated her that Kita and John were scheduled for mediation, and John agreed to counseling. Malik also reminded her that they were all interested in the party, so she'd better send the details.

He knew her too well. Claudia hoped they'd forgotten about how Vicky wanted to meet them, but she had no such luck.

"What's up, baby? You look nervous," Malik asked as she shuffled around him. They were due to be at her parents' place in five minutes. Saturday had arrived, and today was the big day—her father's birthday party. She knew it probably wouldn't start on time, but they would need an additional twenty minutes to pick up Kita and John John.

She scowled at him, but he lifted his hands in surrender. Malik knew Claudia's bad attitude hadn't completely dissolved, no matter how much good dick he gave her—and he stayed giving her good dick. He stood and took the risk to approach her.

He'd been on his best behavior as she dressed in front of him. Malik saw the lingerie underneath the mint green bodycon dress. He told her a few weeks ago how sexy she looked in green, and she'd made it a point to wear the color more often. The short dress put her magnificent legs, and part of her thighs, on display.

The dress featured a cut-out design, which exposed her supple skin from the bottom of her breasts to just above her navel. It may have looked slutty on someone other than Claudia, but she carried herself like a classy, yet fiery queen. He stood behind her and marveled at the way the dress made her ass look. It was round and tight, but concealed just enough so he wouldn't need to fuck someone up.

He stroked her exposed arm and felt her soften immediately under his touch.

"I'm being a bitch, I know." She sagged backward into his embrace. He smelled divine. And his patience with her jitters made her love him that much more.

He turned her so she faced him and looked down into her freshly made-up face. "Damn, you so pretty, with your mean ass." He puckered his lips to kiss her, fully trained on how to do it without ruining her beat.

"I think I love you, Malik Malone."

"I know you do."

He created distance between them, aware she would lose her shit.

"What the hell is that supposed to mean!" she yelled.

He used his long arms to pull her in before she could storm off. "It means I know you're trying to get me to fuck you, yelling at me like this. And I still love you anyway, Claudia Vaughn."

Her breath caught. "You do?"

"Have for a while, but I was waiting for you to say it first." He laughed but was cut off by the thumps from her handbag to his shoulder. "You so damn violent. Come on, girl, and let's go get Kita and nem."

* * *

SOMEHOW, Claudia was able to breathe on the ride from Markita's to her parents'. She thought she would have a burst of anger when John John kept kicking her chair until she remembered something Vicky said about kids and loud noises. She turned on a soundtrack to an animated movie her sister was in last year. It wasn't as big as her coming *Sleeping Dragon* role, but it was popular enough that John John was familiar with it.

Once they arrived and she saw Malik's and Markita's faces, she realized they must have heard the songs a billion times. "Sorry," she said to them as John John continued to sing outside of the car.

They simultaneously kissed their teeth, which Claudia found adorable. They stayed doing twin things.

Delores and Winston approached the group first.

"This must be the man who's been keeping you from us these days," Delores sang.

She was as lovely as she always was. Her gray hair was silk pressed, and she wore a white satin slip dress that made her look a decade younger than she was. Claudia guessed her mother wanted to remind her father, she might be married to a man who was sixty, but she was anything but old.

"I'm Malik. It's a pleasure to meet you, Mrs. Vaughn," Malik said as he grabbed her and pulled her in for a hug.

"Oh my," Delores said. "It's nice to meet you as well." She smoothed her immaculate hair and dress several times before she threw a wink at Claudia.

Winston cleared his throat as he approached. He was a few inches taller than Malik, who was forced to tilt his head upward to meet her father's eyeline.

"Sir, you have a beautiful wife and a beautiful home." Malik stumbled over his words as Winston glared at him.

"I thought you were here with my daughter, not to hit on my wife."

A beat of silence stretched between them, until Winston laughed dryly. "I'm giving you a hard time. Claudy looks happy. I've missed seeing her this way."

While Claudia was relieved her parents seemed to take to Malik, she couldn't help but roll her eyes. They didn't have a track record of acceptance when it came to her.

"And who do we have here?" Delores asked as she stared down at John John—who spun in circles—and Markita who stood beside him.

"This is Malik's twin sister, Markita, and her son, John John," Claudia responded.

Delores's eyes lit up. Her head bounced between the three of them. "I see it now. This little boy is your clone, Malik. And your sister is a girl version of you."

Claudia stepped away. She was afraid she'd embarrass herself in front of Malik if she had to hear her mother's best attempt at sincerity. She heard her mother announce how she was a twin and how they ran in the family.

Victoria sashayed out of the house where everyone was gathered. *Can this day get any worse?* Victoria wore an eerily similar dress as Claudia. The cutouts were in the exact same position, only Vicky's dress flowed to her feet.

"Claudy, why did you copy me?" she asked with a hand propped on her hip.

"Hello to you too, Vicky. And how the hell would I know you had this dress?"

"Because everything always has to be about you." Victoria reached her hand out like she would push Claudia, but Claudia grabbed it and twisted it behind her back. "I'm joking, Claudy." Victoria laughed in a muffled voice. Her head was angled from the sharp pain Claudia's hold had on her.

Everyone had gathered as Claudia released her sister.

"Damn, baby. I thought you was about to knock her out," Malik said.

Victoria's eyes twinkled as she regarded Malik. "You are nothing like I expected. I'm Claudia's prettier sister," she said with a grin as she extended her hand to him.

"I'm Malik. Other than your complexion and attitude, y'all look pretty much the same." Malik scratched the area above his brow uncomfortably. "Congratulations on the new gig."

Surprise covered Victoria's face.

"I can't believe she told you. We haven't had a history of getting along."

"No shit," JW added.

"Watch your language, son," Delores said. She had John John's hand and was headed toward the wooden gazebo in the backyard.

They fell in line behind her mother as Claudia introduced Malik to JW and Victoria to Kita and John John.

"Diamond grill! I thought my sister was gonna get you fired," JW announced out of nowhere.

A hush settled amongst everyone, and confusion covered the faces of Claudia's family.

"She did," Malik said with a smirk. He elbowed her as he filled in JW on how he delivered packages as a temporary job until he could focus on his business. He added, for their entertainment, how he had a different delivery job since Claudia complained and got him fired from the first one, but he'd since forgiven her.

Claudia was finally able to relax. It seemed her family could be on their best behavior. JW and Malik got along almost as well as she enjoyed Kita's company. At one point, JW pulled his sketchbook out and showed John John some of his drawings. JW made comic books for children, but he could draw just about anything. He laid out extra paper and colored pencils for him and Malik's nephew to color while the adults mingled.

Everyone in her family took well to John John. And Claudia had to admit, the crumb snatcher wasn't bad company.

She made her way over to Malik.

"What's up, baby?"

She rolled her eyes, because he knew like she did there was nothing he could do about the thump between her legs. The way he spoke turned her on instantly.

"I have a surprise for you later."

His eyebrows flew up.

"Not that kind of surprise, nasty. I'm taking you somewhere at six."

"If I agree to go, will you let me be nasty after?" He whispered against her ear.

Claudia's face dropped, and Malik whipped around to see who or what was responsible for her dramatic shift.

"Hey, Dad," Tommy said with pride. He walked into the backyard like he'd been invited.

"Hey, son. How have you been?" Winston asked.

At that moment, Claudia hated her dad for the relationship he still had with Tommy. He couldn't have known Tommy put his hands on her, but he was her ex-husband, and everyone knew how hard the divorce was on her.

Tommy had an expensively wrapped gift in his hand and appeared to have had the good sense to attend the party alone. Malik turned and headed in his direction with the slow gait that both scared and turned Claudia on.

"Bruh, what's going on? You look like you about to end somebody." JW was in step with Malik.

"Muthfucka grabbed Claudia and said some shit about how she belong to him whether they divorced or not."

JW's face contorted as Malik's words registered. His head flew in Claudia's direction, who seemed to be frozen in place. His sister, who was known to chew a person up and spit them out, had the body language of a battered woman. What Malik said must have been true.

JW's gait increased, and as he passed Malik, he said, "I got it. Tommy seems like the type to get you locked up. But he won't do shit to me!"

"Winston Jr.!" his mother shrieked.

JW covered his balled fist with his left hand and used the sharpest point of his elbow to smash into the center of Tommy's chest. He kicked Tommy in the balls, and once he fell to the ground, JW stomped him like he was a piece of trash.

"What's gotten into you?" Winston Sr. asked when he was finally able to drag him away.

JW snatched away, enraged as he glared at Tommy. "He grabbed Claudia and wouldn't let her go. I guess he found out about Malik and tried to intimidate her. He said she still *belonged* to him."

"What the hell?" Victoria had made her way over to the commotion.

Claudia recalled how they kept in touch via social media. She looked utterly disgusted. "Bastard!"

Winston craned his neck to find Claudia. "Sweetheart, is this true?"

Claudia nodded. Kita was by her side while the family sorted out the drama with her ex.

Her father gripped Tommy by the collar. "Get off my property. And I expect to hear from your father *tonight*!"

Claudia knew Tommy's father and her father formed and maintained both a business and professional relationship during their marriage. If Winston wanted to make things difficult for the Butners, he could, and Tommy knew it. He left quickly with his tail between his legs.

Malik hung back while Claudia's family checked on her. He was still twisted up about what happened well after the other guests had arrived. JW had saved Tommy's life because whether he used his hands or his weapon, it would've taken the law to get him off once he got started. *Fuck boy!*

His watch told him it was five p.m. Claudia mingled with Kita and the other members of her family. Malik kept his eyes on her as he chopped it up with JW. He liked that kid and hoped he would get to hang out with him more in the future.

Malik swaggered to a bench Claudia and Victoria were perched on. He hadn't wanted to disturb them because they looked so cute together, but he knew she had something planned for six o'clock. Their conversation hushed as he approached, and the two of them took turns giggling.

"What's so funny, baby?"

The girls laughed like his accent was foreign in the state of Georgia. He figured maybe it was in their circle.

"It's cool. You don't have to tell me. I'm glad to see you two getting along."

Claudia reached over and hugged Victoria and made her rounds to say goodbye to her loved ones. Malik said his goodbyes as well and wished Winston a happy birthday. John John was almost asleep but insisted he wanted to stay the night with Ms. Delores. Kita assured him they'd visit again soon.

Thirteen

MALIK AND CLAUDIA hadn't spoken much since the incident with Tommy, but once his sister and nephew were out of the car, it seemed they had to acknowledge the elephant in the room.

She gave him the address of the surprise location so he could plug it into his GPS. The virtual assistant announced they were ten minutes from their destination.

"Are you OK?" Malik asked. His voice was full of concern and laced with frustration.

"Is it bad if I am?"

Malik reached over and grasped her hand. He pulled it to his lips and kissed it.

"No, baby. Not at all."

"What about you?"

"I need to release some aggression." Malik had a toothpick in his mouth, but it hadn't helped.

Claudia unbuckled her seat belt, and Malik swerved. "You serious, baby?"

"As a heart attack." He rubbed his hand down his hair and eyed the time on his dashboard and the freaky look in Claudia's eyes.

"Fuck, baby. We're gonna be late if we stop because I can't do what needs to be done in twenty minutes."

Claudia parted her legs and lifted her dress. Malik moved his eyes to watch her, but he kept his head straight.

"You're making me crazy, girl."

The virtual assistant interrupted Claudia's torture with the news that the destination was on the right.

With most of his blood gone from his brain, Malik asked, "You brought me to a fancy dinner? Am I dressed up enough for this?"

"No. And uh, hell yeah. I would prefer you in a Hood Body Briefs hoodie to this any day."

Malik put the car in park and stared down at himself, confused. "I wore this shit for you." He wore an expensive fitted black shirt tucked into black slacks with a belt. He felt like he was at an athletic press conference.

Claudia smirked. "Thank you, daddy. I appreciate it. You always look good, Malik."

"Yeah, yeah. If I'm not here for dinner, then what am I here for?"

"You'll see. Let's just go."

"Shit, baby. I need a minute to calm down. You was givin' me eyes and lifting your dress and shit."

"OK. I'll see you inside."

Claudia got out of Malik's car with a major surge of adrenaline. She decided to free herself of thoughts of Tommy. Between his beatdown by JW and her father's request to speak to Harold Butner, Tommy's dad, Claudia figured she wouldn't hear another peep from him.

Tonight, she and Malik would sit down with Richard Stoll. He was an affluent man who had made several small businesses household names. Claudia was more than confident in Malik and his brand.

She figured he'd be upset initially about her interference, but once a deal was made, he'd forgive her.

"I'm Claudia Vaughn. I'm here to see Richard Stoll."

"Right this way."

Claudia was escorted past several parties to a quaint VIP area. Only two other tables were occupied in the section. The hostess led her to a table where Nick was seated. *What... the... fuck?* Fury and panic covered her face.

Did she have enough time to verbally kick Nick's ass before Malik appeared? Why the hell was he here? And how could he? He didn't exactly know whose business it was that she wanted to discuss, but that was beside the point.

"Nick?"

He stood and kissed both sides of her cheeks like it was the plan all along. "You look stunning, as usual. I'm sitting in for Richard."

Claudia plopped down in the chair, certain Malik would never forgive her for this ambush.

"Oh."

Before Nick could continue, Malik ambled in her direction. His gait garnered attention from women and men alike. As he took in the scene, Claudia could appreciate his clenched jaw.

"What's he doing here?" Nick asked, mortified. "Why would you bring your boyfriend to a business dinner?"

"Business dinner?" Malik wanted answers. He didn't want shit to do with Nick. *Why the fuck would Claudia say she had a surprise for me that involved Nick's slimy, trying hard to fuck ass?*

"Let me explain," Claudia started. "This meeting was supposed to be with Richard Stoll."

"Richard Stoll that owns the digital marketing conglomerate?" Malik asked, shocking both Claudia and Nick.

"Yeah, baby. That was my surprise." Claudia responded with a wide smile on her face. Malik returned her smile and showcased the diamonds that sparkled in his mouth and made her squirm.

"Wait a minute. He's the guy responsible for the briefs to fit large, athletic built men?" Nick asked.

"Claudia... tell me this old ass muthafucka is not the person you had set this shit up?" Malik hadn't raised his voice, nor had his eyes acknowledged Nick's presence at all.

Claudia bit the inside of her lip nervously.

Malik turned on his heels. "I can't believe you would do this."

She stood and grabbed his arm, but he snatched away from her. She sat back down and glared at Nick. "Why are you really here? Was there ever a meeting scheduled with Stoll?"

Nick didn't respond, and his silence was deafening. "I was eventually going to bring him in."

"You asshole," Claudia whispered. She may have lost the man she loved because Nick thought he could trick her into a work affair. "I don't want anything to do with you."

Nick's face fell, and his shoulders sagged. When he stood, he added, "Don't come crying to me when things don't work out with you two. He's going to bring you down. There's no way he can afford to provide for you the way I can."

Claudia couldn't believe how she'd misjudged him and how Malik had been right about him the entire time. Nick left her there, and she sat astounded and overwhelmed by their exchange.

Tears threatened to fall from her tired eyes. Today had been a long and emotional one. What if Malik didn't want to see her? What if he couldn't forgive her for meddling?

"Excuse me, ma'am," an older woman said from beside her.

Claudia wanted to yell. She wanted to tell her to read the room and fuck off, but she knew better. The lady ate alone and was probably lonely.

"Yes?" Claudia said as she cleared her throat.

"I couldn't help but overhear your conversation."

Claudia willed herself not to roll her eyes. She simply nodded.

"My grandson would love to hear about the business, especially if that attractive man is the current owner. He reminds me of the type of fellow my grandson would love to invest in."

Claudia silently counted to three. This woman's grandson was probably a minister who donated to a business once.

"Wow," Claudia said. She tried to sound enthusiastic but found it hard to focus on the woman's words.

"Do you have Instabook?"

Claudia snickered. "Yes, ma'am." What did she know about Instabook?

The woman opened her phone painfully slow, then aimed it at Claudia. "That's my grandson right there."

Claudia's eyes bulged, and her body perked up. "Taylor Dawn, the owner of Funded by Us clothing, is your grandson?"

"He sure is. He's supposed to meet me for dinner. But he's so busy. He never gets here before dessert." The woman chuckled dryly. "Maybe you could go after the young man and he could meet my Tay Tay."

Claudia nodded like an idiot. If this woman was who she said she was, she had a shot at truly making Malik's dreams come true.

"Would you excuse me for one moment?" Claudia asked as she stood.

"Go get him, hun," the lady said as she waved her hand toward the door.

Claudia rushed to the front of the restaurant and out of the door. She wasn't sure if she should try to call him or get a ride to his parents'. She looked around as if her surroundings would provide an answer, and it did.

Malik stood rested against the side of his car with a fresh toothpick in his mouth. "Took you long enough."

Claudia ran to Malik and jumped in his arms.

"I'm still mad as hell at you," he mumbled. Because Claudia kissed along his face and neck, overjoyed he hadn't left and on cloud nine about her news.

"I know and I'm sorry."

"Let's just go. I don't want to talk about it."

"No," Claudia said in a firm tone and jumped down from his embrace.

"You hungry or something?" Malik sounded deflated, but the good thing was he hadn't given up on her.

"Do you trust me?"

Malik scratched his head and looked around the mostly empty parking lot. Other than the valet, Malik and Claudia seemed to be the only ones outside. Eventually, he nodded.

"OK, good."

"Now what?" Malik asked, irritated.

"We wait."

* * *

TWENTY-SEVEN PAINFUL MINUTES passed before the sleek black limousine arrived. Claudia slapped Malik's arm.

"Damn, girl. You got me out here waiting with no earthly idea why. Now you gonna hit me? You know I'm in love and pussy whipped." Malik shook his head in disgust, but he remained at her side.

"This is the surprise," Claudia said with so much hope in her voice.

"Look, baby—"

"No. This is the surprise to make up for how badly I dropped the ball earlier. Come on."

Claudia dragged Malik with her. They were near the door when the driver got out and opened the passenger door for Taylor Dawn.

Claudia slapped Malik's arm again, but he was speechless. He couldn't believe he was there in the presence of his idol.

Taylor approached Claudia with his hand outstretched. "You must be Claudia. I'm Taylor. It's a pleasure to meet you."

Claudia squealed and was unashamed at her inability to keep her feet on the ground. She jumped up and down and once she was semi-settled, she elbowed Malik in the gut as if he hadn't heard.

"I am. It's so nice to meet you."

"My grandmother said I needed to get over here and meet Claudia and her boyfriend who has a brief idea that is going to make us both rich."

Claudia's head flew in Malik's direction. He wiped his hand down his face several times and accepted Taylor's hand.

"Let's step inside and talk business, my brotha."

As Taylor and his bodyguard walked in, Claudia and Malik followed. Malik grabbed her hand and mouthed, "Thank you, baby. I love your ass so much!"

Epilogue

IT HAD BEEN five months since Malik's meeting with Taylor Dawn. They signed a contract over dessert that night. Hood Body Briefs took off once it was featured on Taylor Dawn's television series, *The Orca Aquarium*, and then it went viral on social media.

Women across the world demanded that men wear Hood Body Briefs if they wanted to make it as their Man Crush Monday. Several professional athletes were pictured in them, and the last Claudia heard, the association for college football wanted to take a meeting with Taylor Dawn and Malik.

Claudia and Malik had also become closer with each other's families. Claudia knew her little brother well, and he'd taken an interest in Kita, but Malik hadn't seemed to notice. There was a tremendous age gap between them, but Claudia could tell the attraction was harmless but mutual. She thought she saw them engrossed in conversation at her dad's birthday party, but was preoccupied with her ex, whose name she no longer spoke.

Victoria was almost done with the *Sleeping Dragon* project. She became the coolest person in the world when she invited John John to watch her work. She was sure to include him in the one in person session she had. He was able to meet the voice behind one of his favorite animated characters. Claudia noticed he hadn't quite accepted that the actor was the cartoon character; he just thought the man sounded a lot like him.

Apparently, *Sleeping Dragon* took longer than most movies because there were children involved. Victoria gave Claudia a hard time when she'd insisted it was further evidence that children ruined everything. Claudia had warmed up to John John and decided even if she didn't like all children, maybe she could get along with a few.

The same couldn't be said for Red. She'd gotten out of her tank for the first-time last month, and Malik almost had a heart attack. He went to use the bathroom in the middle of the night, and there Red was, submerged below the water.

She loved her girl Red but decided to relocate her to JW's to keep the peace. Malik practically lived with her these days, when he wasn't swamped with work. Because of the success of his company, his home would be built ahead of schedule. He told Claudia it was one of his greatest accomplishments, next to his clothing line.

While Malik rose to the challenge when it came to the demands of his new level of success, he hated the excess attention. Malik knew he was a good-looking man, so he wasn't a stranger to a lingering gaze or a bold woman, but the lengths people took to get noticed annoyed the shit out of him. It especially pissed him off when he was with Claudia.

If he had any doubt about whether she was the one for him, the night she connected him with Taylor Dawn sealed the deal. It wasn't just that she'd made it, but it was the way she'd done it. She had so much faith in him and his vision, she distracted him for a half hour until Taylor arrived, after he'd almost broken up with her.

She was his rider. But Malik knew Claudia well enough to know she wasn't interested in a second marriage. And with all his new fame and success, he didn't necessarily want to complicate things. Instead of a proposal, he'd asked her if she'd fuck with him from here on out.

Claudia was tickled and, as usual, turned on. When she asked him what it meant, he replied he bought her something better than a ring. Malik showed her a deposit he made to the women's shelter she regularly donated to.

The deposit would fund The Claudia Vaughn Creative Arts

building for the women to learn or practice creation. He gifted her the official plans for the space where art therapy would be available to the women, along with private lessons and masterclasses with writers, artists, and musicians.

Claudia didn't cry much, but she cried and promptly responded that she would, in fact, fuck with him from here on out. Malik wanted a life partner. He told her if she was open to it, he wanted to file to be domestic partners, and once his home was finished, he wanted her, Kita, and John John to live with them.

Claudia hadn't decided whether she would move in, but Malik assured her she would come around. Not only would she avoid the need to travel for good dick, but she was just as much a part of Hood Body Briefs as he was. She still had her job but had scaled back significantly.

She was honest with her boss and communicated that her decrease in duties was unrelated to her fallout with Nick. Claudia let him know that she was the girlfriend of the creator and owner of Hood Body Briefs. He surprised her when he basically said, "say less."

Malik let Claudia know he'd be in meetings for the day, so Claudia decided to check in with her two-person team, the lowest number she had since she started. As the meeting was in full swing, she heard the loud rattle of a car's bass in front of her home. She tried to ignore it, but it sounded as though the car was parked in her driveway.

The vehicle was stopped, but the owner hadn't tried to lower the volume. Claudia struggled to hear the conversation, so she hid her camera and stomped to the door to investigate the interruption. When she opened the door, her mouth fell open.

"I'm here to deliver a pleasure package," Malik said in his painfully slow and thick southern accent. Malik had an unbuttoned, canary yellow Glamazon uniform top on. His muscles flexed beneath her shocked gaze. She could see the waistband of his tempting Hood Body Briefs peek out from under the fitted black joggers he wore. *Good Lord!*

Claudia finally looked back up into the diamond studded smile of the man of her dreams. "I'm going to need to hop off," she said into her headphones.

"You talking to me?" Malik's eyes twinkled in delight. He was proud of himself for his impromptu role playing.

She held up her hand to hush him. "Not you! And where's my package?"

Malik backed her into the house and lifted her. "I'm right here, baby."

The End

Afterword

Thank you for finishing The Pleasure Package.

If you enjoyed Malik and Claudia's story, please **leave a positive review on Amazon** and **TikTok** and share it with your friends.

Also, be sure to show my Facebook like page some love with a like and follow!

https://www.facebook.com/DeniseEssex222

Thank you in advance,
Denise Essex

DENISE ESSEX

Connect with Denise

Sign up for my mailing list for sexy surprises, discounted erotic products, and a taste of my latest juicy project 💋 You'll also be the first to learn whose story is up next.

Mailing List: http://eepurl.com/h15QoD
Readers Group: https://www.facebook.com/groups/deniseessexheat-seekers
Amazon Author Page: https://www.amazon.com/author/denise_essex
Facebook page: https://www.facebook.com/DeniseEssexAuthor
INSTAGRAM: https://www.instagram.com/deniseessex222/
@DeniseEssex222
YouTube: https://www.youtube.com/channel/UCFtlvIsLaQy1lF1R6RNiNiQ
TikTok: @DeniseEssex222
Twitter: @DeniseEssex222

Thank You

Thanks for reading! If you enjoyed this book, please leave a review on Amazon and mark it as read on Goodreads. We hate errors but they do happen. If you catch any, please send them to us directly at blovepublications@gmail.com with ERRORS as the subject.